A VALENTINE TO REMEMBER
One day they will never forget!

A DATE WITH HER VALENTINE DOC
by Melanie Milburne

Bertie Clark really *shouldn't* be fantasising about
Dr Matt Bishop—he's her boss, and is 100%
off limits! But, working on the hospital's St
Valentine's Day Ball with him, Bertie knows she
can't ignore the sparks flying around
for ever—surely a girl deserves a little fun?

IT HAPPENED IN PARIS…
by Robin Gianna

Biochemical engineer Avery Girard might have
sworn off men, but she can't help but get
swept away by the beauty, magic and romance
of Valentine's Day in Paris…especially when
she's spending it with totally irresistible
Dr Jack Dunbar. One little fling can't hurt, *right*?

**Fall in love this Valentine's Day
with these sparkling romances
available from February 2015!**

Dear Reader

When my editor suggested I write a book set in Paris with a Valentine theme, I loved the idea! After all, what could possibly be more romantic than my hero and heroine meeting in Paris and falling in love (even if they know they shouldn't)?

I had such fun researching Paris and things to do there—though I admit it was a bit of a challenge that it had to be set in February! No spring trees bursting into bloom, no lazing in sunshiny parks lush with the scent of roses, no warm weather strolls along the Seine…

But I managed to find other things for Jack and Avery to enjoy when they first meet—including succumbing to a brief fling! He's an interventional cardiologist and she's a biomedical engineer—you can imagine their shock when they discover they'll be colleagues on the clinical trial they're in Paris to conduct. A trial that's extremely important to both of them.

Jack never mixes business with pleasure. Avery knows they might very possibly end up with different opinions on how the research is going. What will happen if Jack finds out that she holds the entire future of his trial in her hands?

If you enjoy Jack and Avery's story I'd love to hear from you! Find me on Facebook, Twitter, or my website: www.robingianna.com

Robin xoxo

IT HAPPENED
IN PARIS…

BY
ROBIN GIANNA

Published in Great Britain 2015
by Mills & Boon, an imprint of Harlequin (UK) Limited,
Eton House, 18-24 Paradise Road, Richmond, Surrey, TW9 1SR

© 2015 Robin Gianakopoulos

ISBN: 978-0-263-25935-3

Harlequ...
renewa... MORAY COUNCIL ...wn grow...   ...n
sustain... LIBRARIES & ...form
to the l... ...of the ...of origin
            INFO.SERVICES
Printed...
by CPI...

After completing a degree in journalism, working in the advertising industry, then becoming a stay-at-home mum, **Robin Gianna** had what she calls her 'midlife awakening'. She decided she wanted to write the romance novels she'd loved since her teens, and embarked on that quest by joining RWA, Central Ohio Fiction Writers, and working hard at learning the craft.

She loves sharing the journey with her characters, helping them through obstacles and problems to find their own happily-ever-afters. When not writing, Robin likes to create in her kitchen, dig in the dirt, and enjoy life with her tolerant husband, three great kids, drooling bulldog and grouchy Siamese cat.

To learn more about her work visit her website: www.robingianna.com

Recent titles by Robin Gianna:

FLIRTING WITH DR OFF-LIMITS
THE LAST TEMPTATION OF DR DALTON
CHANGED BY HIS SON'S SMILE

For my wonderful children, Arianna, James and George.
You three are truly the light of my life.

A big thank you to good friend Steven J. Yakubov, MD,
who has been conducting TAVI clinical trials overseas
and now in the US for years, and who inspired this story.
I so appreciate it, Steve, that you called me to answer
all my questions even after you'd had
almost no sleep for three nights. Thanks bunches!

**Praise for
Robin Gianna:**

'If you're looking for a story sweet but
exciting, characters loving but cautious,
a fan of Medical Romances™ or looking for a story
to try to see if you like the medical genre,
CHANGED BY HIS SON'S SMILE is the story
for you! I would never have guessed Robin
is a debut author: the story flowed brilliantly,
the dialogue was believable and I was
thoroughly engaged in the medical dramas.'
—*Contemporary Romance Reviews*

CHAPTER ONE

JACK DUNBAR STUDIED the map in his hand, trying to figure out where the heck he was in this city of two million people. He was determined not to waste his first hours in Paris, and never mind that he'd only had a few hours of sleep while folded into an airplane seat, couldn't speak French and had no idea how to get around.

But, hey, a little adventure never hurt anyone. Even getting lost would be a welcome distraction from thinking about the presentation he had to give tonight. The presentation that would begin the new phase of his career he'd worked so hard for. The presentation that would launch the newest medical device, hopefully save lives and change forever the way heart-valve replacement surgery was performed.

Before any sightseeing, though, the first thing on his list was coffee and a little breakfast. Jack stepped into the hotel restaurant and saw that a huge buffet was set up just inside the open doors. Silver chafing dishes, mounds of breads and cheeses, fruits and you-name-it covered an L-shaped table, but the thought of sitting there eating a massive breakfast alone wasn't at all appealing. He approached the maître d'. "Excuse me. Is there just a small breakfast I can grab somewhere?"

"Voilà!" The man smiled and waved his arm at the buffet with a flourish. *"Le petit déjeuner!"*

Jack nearly laughed. If that was the small breakfast, he'd hate to see a big one. "Thank you, but I want just coffee and something quick. What's nearby?"

"Everything you could wish for is right here, *monsieur.*"

"Yes, I see that, but—"

"I know a little place that's just what you're looking for," a feminine voice said from behind him. "When in France, eat like the French do. And that spread in there is most definitely meant for Americans."

He turned, and a small woman with the greenest eyes he'd ever seen stood there, an amused smile on her pretty face. He smiled back, relieved that someone might actually steer him in the right direction, and that she not only spoke English, but sounded like she was American, too. "That's exactly what I want. To immerse myself in French culture for a while. And soon, because I need a cup of coffee more than I need oxygen right now."

Those amazing eyes, framed by thick, dark lashes, sparkled as her smile grew wider. "Caffeine is definitely the number one survival requirement. Come on."

Leaving barely a second for him to thank the unhelpful maître d', she wrapped her hand around his biceps and tugged him toward the door and out into the chilly January streets of Paris. "Just down the street is the perfect café. We can get coffee and a baguette, then we'll be good to go."

We? Jack had to grin at the way she'd taken over. Not that he minded. Being grabbed and herded down the street by a beautiful woman who obviously knew a little about Paris was a pleasure he hadn't expected, but was more than happy about.

"I'm Avery, by the way."

"Jack." He looked at her and realized her unusual name went well with a very unusual woman. A woman who took a perfect stranger down the street to a coffee shop as though she'd known him for days instead of seconds. A red wool hat was pulled onto her head, covering lush dark brown hair that spilled from beneath it. A scarf of orange, red and yellow was wrapped around her neck and tucked inside a short black coat, and tight-fitting black pants hugged her shapely legs. On her feet she wore yellow rain boots with red ducks all over them, and a purple umbrella was tucked under her arm. Dull she most definitely was not.

"Nice to meet you, Jack." Her smile was downright dazzling. The morning looked a whole lot brighter than it had a few moments ago, despite the sky being as gray as pencil lead. "How do you like your coffee? American style? If you really want to be French, you'll have to drink espresso. But I won't judge you either way."

Her green eyes, filled with a teasing look, were so mesmerizing he nearly stumbled off the curb when they crossed the street. "Somehow I think that's a lie. And while I can handle being judged, I like espresso."

"I knew you were a man after my own heart."

He'd be willing to bet a lot of men were after her heart and a whole lot more.

The little coffee shop smelled great, and he followed Avery to the counter. She ordered in French, and the way the words slipped from her tongue, it sounded to him like she spoke the language nearly like a native.

"You ordered, so I'm paying," he said.

"That's what I was hoping for. Why else did you think I brought you along?"

"And here I thought it was my good looks and sophistication."

"I did find that, combined with your little-boy-lost look, irresistible, I must admit."

He chuckled. Damned if she wasn't about the cutest woman he'd been around in a long time. They took their baguettes and tiny cups of espresso to a nearby tall table and stood. Jack nearly downed his cup of hot, strong coffee in one gulp. "This is good. Just what I needed. Except there isn't nearly enough of it."

"I know. And I even ordered us double shots. I always have to get used to the tiny amounts of espresso they serve when I'm in Europe. We Americans are used to our bottomless cups of coffee."

"Are you here as a tourist? With friends?" Jack couldn't imagine she was traveling alone, but hoped she was. Maybe they could spend some time together, since he'd be in Paris for an entire month. With any luck, she was living here.

"I'm in Paris to work, and I'm alone. How about you?"

"Me, too. Working and alone. But I do have a few hours to kill today. Any chance you'll show me around a little in exchange for me buying lunch?"

"We're eating breakfast, and you're already thinking about lunch?" More of that teasing look, and he found himself leaning closer to her. Drawn to her. "I've already proved I plan my friendships around who'll buy. So the answer is yes."

He smiled. Maybe this great start to his trip to Paris was a good omen. "Where to first? I know nothing about Paris except the Eiffel Tower, which I know is close because I saw it from the hotel."

"Paris is a wonderful city for walking. Even though it's cold today and may well rain. Or even snow. Let's walk toward the Seine and go from there. If we hit the tower early, we'll avoid some of the crazy lines."

"There are lines this time of year? I didn't think there would be many tourists."

"There are always tourists. Not as many in January and February as in spring and summer, but still plenty. Lots come to celebrate Valentine's Day in Paris. Romantic, you know?"

He didn't, really. Sure, he'd had women in his life, some briefly and some for a little longer. But, like his father in the past and his brother now, his life was about work. Working to help patients. Working to save people like his grandfather, who'd had so much to live for but whose heart had given out on him far too soon.

Avery finished her last bite of bread and gathered up her purse and umbrella, clearly ready to move on.

"I don't suppose they give little to-go cups of espresso, do they?" he asked.

"You suppose right," she said with a grin. "The French don't believe in multitasking to quite the same degree we do. They'd shake their heads at crazy Americans who eat and drink while walking around the city."

"I'll have to get a triple shot at lunch, then," he said as they stood. He resisted the urge to lick the last drop from his cup, figuring Avery wouldn't be too impressed. Might even come up with an excuse not to take him to the Eiffel Tower, and one drop of coffee wasn't anywhere near worth that risk.

They strolled down cobbled streets and wide walks

toward the tower, Avery's melodic voice giving him a rundown of various sights as they strolled. Not overly chatty, just the perfect combination of information and quiet enjoyment. Jack's chest felt light. Spending this time with her had leeched away all the stress he'd been feeling, all the intense focus on getting this study off the ground, to the exclusion of everything. How had he gotten so lucky as to have her step into his first day in France exactly when he'd needed it?

"That's L'Hôtel des Invalides," she said, pointing at a golden building not too far away. "Napoleon is buried there. I read that they regilded the dome on the anniversary of the French Revolution with something like twenty pounds of gold. And I have to wonder. Wouldn't all that gold have been better used to drape women in jewelry?"

"So you like being draped in gold?" He looked at the silver hoops in her ears and silver bangles on her wrist. Sexy, but not gold, and not over the top in any way.

"Not really. Though if a man feels compelled to do that, who am I to argue?" She grinned and grasped his arm again. "Let's get to the tower before the crowds."

She picked up the pace as they walked the paths crisscrossing a green expanse in front of the tower. Considering how cold it was, a surprising number of people were there snapping pictures and standing in line as they approached. "Are you afraid of heights?"

"Who, me? I'm not afraid of anything."

"Everyone's afraid of something." Her smiling expression faded briefly into seriousness before lightening again. "Obviously, the Eiffel Tower is super tall, and the elevators can be claustrophobic even while you're thinking how scary it is to be going so high. I'll hold your hand, though, if you need me to."

"You know, I just might be afraid after all."

She laughed, and her small hand slid into his. Naturally. Just like it belonged there.

"Truth? I get a little weirded out on the elevator," she said in a conspiratorial tone. "So if I squeeze your hand too tight, I'm sorry."

"I'm tough, don't worry."

"I bet you are." She looked up at him with a grin. "The lines aren't too bad, but let's take the stairs anyway."

He stared at her in disbelief. "The stairs?"

"You look like you're probably fit enough." Her green eyes laughed at whatever the heck his expression was. "But we don't take them all the way to the top. Just to the second level, and we'll grab the elevator there. Trust me, it's the best way to see everything, especially on a day like today, when it gets cloudier the higher you go."

"So long as we don't have to spend the entire day climbing, I'm trusting you, Ms. Tour Guide. Lead the way." The stairs were surprisingly wide and the trek up sent his heart beating faster and his breath shorter. Though maybe that was just from being with Avery. For some inexplicable reason, she affected him in a way he couldn't quite remember feeling when he first met a woman.

They admired the views from both the first and second levels, Avery pointing out various landmarks, before they boarded the glass elevator. People were mashed tightly inside, but Jack didn't mind being forced to stand so close to Avery. To breathe in her appealing scent that was soft and subtle, a mix of fresh air and light perfume and her.

The ride most definitely would challenge anyone with either of the fears Avery had mentioned, the view through the crisscrossed metal of the tower incredible as they soared above Paris. On the viewing platform at the top, the cold wind whipped their hair and slipped inside Jack's coat, and he wrapped his arm around her shoulders to try to keep her warm.

"You want to look through the telescope? Though we won't be able to see too far with all the clouds," she said, turning to him. Her cheeks were pink, her beautiful lips pink, too, and, oh, so kissable. Her hair flew across her face, and Jack lifted his fingers to tuck it beneath her hat, because he couldn't resist feeling the softness of it between his fingers.

"I want to look at you, mostly," he said, because it was true. "But I may never get up here again, so let's give it a try."

Her face turned even more pink at his words before she turned to poke a few coins in the telescope. They took turns peering through it, and her face was so close to his he nearly dipped his head to kiss her. Starting with her cheek, then, if she didn't object, moving on from there to taste her mouth. Their eyes met in front of the telescope, and her tongue flicked out to dampen her lips, as if she might be thinking of exactly the same thing.

He stared in fascination as her pupils dilated, noting flecks, both gold and dark, within the emerald green of her eyes. He slowly lowered his head, lifted his palm to her face and—

"Excuse me. You done with the telescope?" a man asked, and Avery took a few steps back.

"We're all done," she said quickly. The heat he hoped he'd seen in her expression immediately cooled to a friendly smile. "Ready to go, Jack? I think we've seen all there is to see from up here today."

Well, damn. Kissing her in the middle of that crowd wasn't the best idea anyway, but even the briefest touch of her lips on his would have been pretty sweet, he knew. "I'm ready."

They crammed themselves onto the elevator once more, though it wasn't quite as packed as it had been on the way up. He breathed in her scent again as he tucked a few more strands of hair under her hat. "Thanks for bringing me up here. That was amazing." *She* was amazing. "So what now, Ms. Tour Guide? Time for lunch?"

"There you go, thinking about food again." She gave him one of her cute, teasing looks. "But I admit I'm getting a little hungry, too. There's a great place just a little way along the river I like. There will be a few different courses, but don't worry—it won't break your wallet."

He didn't care what it cost. Getting to spend a leisurely lunch with Avery was worth a whole lot of money.

They moved slowly down a tree-lined path by the river, and he felt the most absurd urge to hold her hand again. As though they'd known each other a lot longer than an hour or two. Which reminded him he still hardly knew anything about her at all. "Do you live here? You obviously speak French well," he said.

"My parents both worked in France for a while, and I went to school here in Paris for two years. You tend to learn a language fast that way. I'm just here for a month or so this time."

"What do you do?"

"I— Oh!" As though they'd stepped out from beneath a shelter, heavy sheets of rain mixed with thick, wet snowflakes suddenly poured on their heads, and Avery fumbled with her umbrella to get it open. It was small, barely covering both their heads. Jack had to hunch over since she was so much shorter than him as, laughing, they pressed against one another to try to stay dry.

He maneuvered the two of them under a canopy of trees lining the river and had to grin. The Fates were handing him everything today, including a storm that brought him into very close contact with Avery. Exactly where he wanted to be.

He lifted his finger to slip a melting snowflake from her long lashes. "And here I'd pictured Paris as sunny, with beautiful flowers everywhere. I didn't even know it snowed here."

"You can't have done your homework." Her voice was breathy, her mouth so close to his he got a little breathless, too. "It rains and snows here a lot. Parisians despise winter with a very French passion."

He didn't know about French passion. But hadn't Avery said when in France, do as the French do? He more than liked the idea of sharing some passion with Avery. "I'm not a big fan of winter, either, when snow and ice make it harder getting to and from work."

"Ah, that sounds like you must be a workaholic." She smiled, her words vying for attention with the pounding rain on the nylon above them.

"That accusation would probably be accurate. I spend pretty much all my time at work."

"I must have caught you at a good moment, then, since you're sightseeing right now. Or, at least, we were sightseeing before we got stuck in this."

"You did catch me at a good moment." Maybe the romantic reputation of Paris was doing something to him, because he lifted his hands to cup her cheeks. Let his fingers slip into her hair that cascaded from beneath her hat. After all, what better place to kiss a beautiful woman than under an umbrella by the Seine in the shadow of the Eiffel Tower? "I'm enjoying this very good moment."

Her eyes locked with his. He watched her lips part, took that as the invitation he was looking for and lowered his mouth to hers.

The kiss was everything he'd known it would be. Her sexy lips had tormented him the entire time they'd been together in that elevator and standing close to one another on the observation deck. Hell, they'd tormented him just minutes after they'd met as he'd watched her nibble her baguette and sip her espresso. He could still faintly taste the coffee on her lips and an incredible sweetness that was her alone.

He pulled back an inch, to see how she was feeling about their kiss. If she thought it was as amazing as he did. If she'd be all right with another, longer exploration. Her eyes were wide, her cheeks a deep pink as she stared at him, but thankfully she didn't pull away and he went back for more.

He'd intended to keep it sweet, gentle, but the little gasp that left her mouth and swirled into his own had him delving deeper, all sense of anything around them gone except for the unexpected intimacy of this kiss they were sharing. Her slim hand came up to cradle his neck. It was cold, and soft, and added another layer of delicious sensation to the moment, and he had to taste more of her rain-moistened skin. Wondered if she'd possibly let him taste more than her face and throat. If she'd let him explore every inch of what he knew would be one beautiful body on one very special, beautiful afternoon.

Lost in sensory overload, Avery's eyelids flickered, then drifted shut again as Jack's hot mouth moved from her lips to slide across her chilled cheek. Touched the hollow of her throat, her jaw, the tender spot beneath her ear. She'd never kissed a man she'd just met before, but if it was always this good, she planned to keep doing it. And doing it. And doing it.

His hands cupping her cheeks were warm, and his breath that mingled with her own was warm, too, as he brought his mouth back to hers. Her heart pounded in her ears nearly as hard as the rain on the umbrella. She curled one hand behind his neck, hanging on tight before her wobbly knees completely gave way and she sank to the ground to join the water pooling around their feet.

The sensation of cold rain and snow splattering over her face had her opening her eyes and pulling her mouth from his. Dazed, she realized she'd loosened her grip on the umbrella, letting it sway sideways, no longer protecting them. Jack grasped the handle to right it, holding it above their heads again, his dark brown eyes gleaming. His black hair, now a shiny, wet ebony, clung to his forehead. Water droplets slid down his temple.

"Umbrellas don't work too well hanging upside down. Unless your goal is to collect water instead of repel it," he said, a slow smile curving the sexy lips that had made her lose track of exactly where they were. Lips that had traveled deliciously across several inches of her skin until she nearly forgot her own name.

"I know. Sorry." She cleared her throat, trying to gather her wits. "Except you didn't bring an umbrella at all, so you would have gotten wet anyway."

"True. Not that I mind. I like watching the raindrops track down your cute nose and onto your pretty lips." His finger reached out to trace the parts he'd just mentioned, lingering at her mouth, and she nearly licked the raindrops from his finger until she remembered a few very important things.

Things like the fact that she barely knew him. Like the fact that they were standing in a public place. Like the fact that she wasn't looking for a new relationship to replace the not-good one she'd only recently left.

She stared at the silkiness of his dark brows and the thickness of his black lashes, all damp and spiky from the rain. At the water dripping from his hair, over a prominent cheekbone, down the hollow of his cheek and across his stubborn-looking jaw. The thought crossed her mind that she'd never, ever spent time with a man so crazily good-looking. Even more good-looking than her ex-boyfriend, Kent, and she'd thought at the time he was a god in the flesh. At least for a while, until she'd figured out the kind of overly confident and egotistical guy he really was. Until she'd found out he was actually the one convinced he was godlike.

Getting it on again so soon with another man was not something she planned on doing.

She drew a deep breath. Time to bring some kind of normalcy to a very abnormal day. "Let's go to the café, dry off a little and get some food. You being Mr. Hungry and all."

"I've realized there's only one thing I'm hungry for at the moment." His lips moved close to hers again as his eyes, all smoldering and intense, met hers. "You. All of you."

All of her? Was he saying what she thought he was saying? She tried to think of a quick, light response and opened her mouth to speak, but no words came out. Maybe because she could barely breathe.

He kissed one corner of her mouth, then the other. "What do you say we head to the hotel for a while? A little dessert before lunch. I want a better taste of you."

Her heart leaped into her throat. Never having kissed a man she didn't know also meant never having had a quick fling with one. Never dreamed she ever would. But something about the way he was looking at her, the way his fingers were softly stroking her cheek and throat, something about the way her body quivered from head to toe and heat pooled between her legs had her actually wondering if maybe today was the day to change that.

After all, her last two relationships had ended with loud, hurtful thuds. Didn't she deserve some no-strings fun, just this once? She'd only be in Paris for one month, busy at work most of the time. The perfect setup for exactly what he was suggesting. And what would be the harm of enjoying what she knew would be one exciting, memorable afternoon with an exciting, memorable man?

"I…um…" She stopped talking and licked her lips,

gathering the courage to shove aside her hesitation and just say yes.

"I know. We've just met, and it's not something I usually do, either. Honest." He cupped her cheeks with his cold hands and pressed a soft kiss to her mouth. "But being with you here in Paris just feels right. Doesn't it? It just feels damned right."

She found herself nodding, because it did. For whatever crazy reason, it felt all too right. A no-strings, nothing-serious, no-way-to-get-hurt moment with a super-sexy man to help her forget all about her past disappointments.

Another drop of water slid over her eyelid, distracting her from all those thoughts, and she swiped it away. "Except I'm all wet, you know."

The second the words left her mouth his eyes got all hot and devilish, and she felt herself flush, realizing what she'd said. "That's a plus, not a problem."

A breathless laugh left her lips. Before she could change her mind she decided to give herself a little present to make up for what she'd been through with her past jerky boyfriends.

Silent communication must have zinged between them, because they grasped one another's hands and headed in a near run to the hotel. To her surprise, the closer they got, the more excited she felt. She was entering unknown territory here, and hadn't she always promised herself she'd live life as an adventure? Plunging into bed with Jack for an hour or two seemed sure to be one thrilling adventure.

With her heart thumping so hard she feared he could hear it, Avery followed Jack as he shoved open the door to his hotel room. Once inside, the nervous butterflies she'd expected to flap around earlier finally showed up. She stared at him, hands sweating, as he shut the door behind her, trying to think of what the heck she should say or do now that they were actually here.

"Wouldn't you know that the minute we come inside, it stops raining?" she said lamely. Why was she so suddenly, crazily nervous? A little fling was no big deal, right? People probably did things like sleeping with someone they barely knew all the time. Especially in Paris. She didn't, but surely plenty of women did.

"Maybe if we're lucky, it'll start raining again when we go out. I like kissing it off you." The brown eyes that met hers held amusement and a banked-down hint of the passion that had scorched between them just minutes ago.

He shut the door and flipped the lock, his gaze never leaving hers. The heat and promise and that odd touch of amusement in the dark depths of his gaze all sent her heart into a little backflip before he pulled her into his arms and kissed her.

Unlike their previous kiss, this one didn't start out soft and slow. It was hard and intense, his tongue teasing hers until she forgot all about what she should say or do. Forgot where they were. Forgot to breathe. His fingers cupped the back of her head, tangled in her hair, as the kiss got deeper, wilder, pulling a moan from her chest that might have been embarrassing if she'd been able to think at all.

His mouth left hers, moving hot and moist to the side of her neck to nuzzle there. "You feeling more relaxed now?" he murmured.

How had he known? Though relaxed probably wasn't

quite the right word to describe how she was feeling. "Um, yes. Thank you."

He eased back, his fingers reaching for the buttons of her coat and undoing every one of them before she'd had a chance to blink. "I don't know about you, but I'm feeling a little warm," he said as he slipped it from her shoulders and tossed it on a chair.

"Must be from all that running to the hotel," she said, breathless, but not from their fast trek to his room. "I figured it was a good chance to start training for the spring marathon."

His lips curved. "I thought we were running for a different reason." This time, his hands reached for the buttons of her blouse, the backs of his fingers skimming her skin and making it tingle as he slowly undid them one by one. "The reason being that I can't wait to see what you're wearing under this."

Her lacy white blouse dipped low over her breasts, and pure, feminine pleasure swept through her at the way his eyes darkened as he stared down at them. At the way a deep whoosh of breath left his lungs. His fingertips slipped down her collarbone and inside her bra to cup her breast at the same time that his mouth covered hers.

Oh. My. The man was certainly one amazing kisser. World class, really, and her bones nearly melted at the sensations swirling around her. His cool hand on her breast, her nipples tightening into his palm. His hot mouth tracking along her skin, her bra now slipping completely off her to the floor. Her pants somehow magically loose enough to allow his other wide palm to slide inside to grasp her rear before it moved to the front and touched her moist folds, making her gasp.

The loud patter of rain again on the window had him pausing his intimate exploration, and he lifted his head, his dark eyes gleaming. "Guess it's a good thing we came in here out of the rain."

"Good thing," she managed before he resumed kissing and touching her until she was trembling with the intense pleasure of it all.

"Avery." The way he said her name in a rough whisper, the way he expertly moved his fingers while kissing her mouth and face and throat, had her nearly moaning. It all felt so wonderful, every bit of nervousness evaporated, replaced by want and need.

How she ended up on the bed she couldn't say, but when his mouth left hers she looked at him, foggily realizing that she was somehow flat on her back completely naked, while he stood there, staring at her.

"You are every bit as beautiful as I'd fantasized you'd be," he said. "Looking at you takes my breath away."

If that was true, then neither of them had much of an ability to breathe at the moment.

"My turn to look at you. Strip, please."

Those bold words coming out of her mouth shocked her, but he just laughed. "Your wish is my command." His gaze stayed on her as he quickly yanked off his shirt, and her breath caught at his lean but muscular torso. As he shoved off his pants, his erection became fully, impressively but all too briefly visible before his body covered hers, hot and deliciously heavy.

"You didn't give me much time to look at you," she managed to say.

"Sorry. Couldn't wait to feel all your gorgeous, soft skin against all of mine."

Well, if he put it that way. She had to admit it did feel amazingly, wonderfully, delectably good.

Was she really doing this? Lying naked with a man she barely knew? The feel of his body on hers, his mouth pressing sweet kisses to everything within reach of it, his smooth, warm skin beneath her hands told her the answer was yes, but to her surprise she didn't feel tense or strange or regretful. All she felt was toe-curl-ingly excited and turned on.

His hands and mouth roamed everywhere until she found herself making little sounds and moving against him in a way that would have been embarrassing if she hadn't been so totally absorbed in the sensations and how he made her feel. Nearing orgasm more times than she could count before he backed off and slowed things down, she was close to begging him when he finally rolled on a condom, grasped her hips with his hands and pulled her to him.

Instinctively, she wrapped her legs around his waist, inviting him in, and the way they moved together made her think, in the tiny recess of her brain that could still function, that it seemed impossible they'd met only that morning. That this dance they danced hadn't been etched in both their bodies and minds many a time be-fore.

And when she cried out, it was his name on her lips and hers on his as they fell together.

CHAPTER TWO

"JUST SO YOU KNOW…it's really true that I don't usually do this." Her pulse and breathing finally slowing to near normal, Avery managed to drag the sheet up to cover her breasts. She glanced over at Jack, whose head lay on the pillow next to hers, eyes closed, looking as sated and satisfied as she felt. She wasn't sure why the words had tumbled out, but once they had, she wasn't sorry. She didn't want Jack to think she routinely picked up men, showed them around, then dove into bed with them.

"Do what?"

The expression on his face was one of bland innocence, completely at odds with the amused glint in the eyes that slowly opened to look at her. She couldn't help but make an impatient sound. "You know very well what. Sleep with men I've just met. Heck, I've never even kissed a man I just met."

He rolled to his side, his warm body pressing against hers. "I believe it was I who kissed you. Figured it was a Parisian tradition. The city of romance and everything. And what's more romantic than a rainstorm in the shadow of the Eiffel Tower?"

"Well. There is that." Though she was pretty confident that if it had been any other man she'd invited to breakfast that morning, there wouldn't have been any kissing on their trek around town or any rolling around in the sheets, complete with a lovely afterglow. And, to her surprise, no feelings of regret at all. Maybe because she knew it would happen just this once.

The moment she'd stepped off the hotel elevator that morning, her attention had gone straight to him like a magnet. Tall, lean and obviously American, with an adorably befuddled expression on his handsome face as he'd spoken to the maître d', she'd moved toward him without thinking, inviting a stranger for coffee and breakfast as though she did it every day. Which he doubtless assumed she did.

"I hope you're not regretting it. Our kiss, and now this." He propped himself up on his elbow and slowly stroked his finger down her cheek. "I know I don't. Being so close to you under that umbrella, there was no way I could stop myself. And once I'd kissed you, all I could think of was kissing you more."

No way she could have resisted his kiss, either. Or the bliss that had come afterward. Not that she'd tried at all. "Well," she said again, as though the word might somehow finalize the whole crazy afternoon, "we've shared *le petit déjeuner*, walked a bit of the city and gone up the tower. Kissed under an umbrella and made love while it rained outside. I guess it's a good time to find out a little about each other. I hope you're not married?"

She said it jokingly, but a small part of her suddenly wondered if he possibly could be. If he was the type of man who philandered when working out of town. Her stomach clenched at the thought. After all, she knew that type way more intimately than she wished she did. Would Jack admit it if he was?

"Not married. Never have been. Remember, I told you, all I do is work. Which probably makes me pretty boring."

Whew. She looked at him carefully and managed to relax. Surely no one could lie about a wife so convincingly. "Don't worry, you're not completely boring." His twinkling dark eyes and devilish smile proved he knew he was darned exciting to be around. "Tell me something else about you. What's your favorite food? Besides espresso, that is."

"Sorry, coffee definitely is number one on my list of life's sustenance. Though I'm sure anything licked from your lips would qualify, too."

She laughed and shook her head. "I don't have to ask you about talents, because I already know a few of them. Blarney being one."

"And my other talents?" His eyes gleamed as his wide hand splayed on her back, pressing her close against him, and the heat of his skin on hers made her short of breath all over again.

"I'm not stroking your ego any bigger than it already is."

"How about stroking something else, then?"

"Already did that. And I see I'll have to watch what I say around you."

He chuckled as he kissed her shoulder, and she found herself thinking about his mouth and those talents of his and wasn't sure if it was that or his body heat making her feel so overly warm. Again. "So what are your hobbies?" he asked.

"I don't know if I'd call it a hobby, but I like to run.

Helps clear my mind when it gets too busy. And I like marshmallows. A lot."

"Marshmallows?" He laughed out loud at that. "You're kidding."

"Unfortunately, no. I pop the little ones when I'm working on the computer. Which is why I have to run. Don't want to *become* a marshmallow."

"You're about as far from a marshmallow as anyone could be." His hand stroked feather-light up her arm and across her chest to slide down the other, making her quiver. "I'd like to run more than just on a treadmill, but my work just doesn't leave me that kind of time."

"So what is this work you spend all your time doing?"

"I'm a cardiologist."

Every muscle froze, and her breath stopped as she stared at him. A cardiologist? *Cardiologist?* Could this really be happening?

He was probably used to women swooning when he announced that, but not her. She'd worked with more cardiologists than she cared to think about, and being arrogant and egotistical seemed to be a requirement for becoming that kind of specialist. Something she'd allowed herself to forget for too long with her last two boyfriends.

Along with her shock came another, even more chilling thought, which now seemed all too likely since they were staying at the same hotel. Her heart thumped hard in her chest, her body now icy cold as she tugged the sheet up tighter around it. "What's your last name, Jack?"

"Dunbar." He smiled, obviously not sensing the neon "oh, crap" vibes she had to be sending off. "I'm work-

ing for the next month at the Saint Malo Hospital, testing a new heart-valve replacement device. I've worked
damned hard to get the design finished and to get the
arrangements for the trial finalized. Can't believe it's
finally about to happen."

Oh. My. Lord. She couldn't quite believe it, either.
Not the trial starting. This unbelievable coincidence.

How was it possible that the man she'd just slept with
was Dr. Jack Dunbar? The Jack Dunbar she'd be working with and observing at the hospital? The Jack Dunbar who was testing the procedure many, including her,
hoped would someday always be used, instead of open-
heart surgery, to replace faulty heart valves? The Jack
Dunbar who had helped develop the next generation of
valve replacement catheter based on her original design?

A next generation she feared wasn't any better, or
safer, than her own had been.

And if it became necessary to voice her opinion that
the trial should be halted, he wouldn't feel like kissing
her or making love with her again, that was for sure.
Not that she planned on more kisses and lovemaking,
anyway.

A cardiologist was the absolute last kind of man she
wanted in her life. Again.

"How about you?" He lay back, reaching to grasp
her hand, his thumb brushing against her skin. Just as it
had earlier when they'd been walking in such a lovely,
companionable way. This time the feeling it gave her
wasn't electrifying and sweet. The sensation felt more
like discomfort and dismay. "So, what kind of last name
goes with Avery? And what kind of work brings you
to Paris?"

She swallowed hard. "Funny you should ask. My work has a lot to do with your own, Dr. Dunbar."

"Your work is similar to mine?" Jack asked, obvious surprise etched on his face. "In what way? Are you a doctor?"

"No. I have a doctorate in biomedical engineering." She left it at that, which was absurd, since it was all going to come out sooner or later, and it might as well be now. Lying naked in bed with him.

That realization had her shaking off her stunned paralysis to leap out of bed and grab up her clothes.

"That's…impressive." He propped himself up on his elbow, obviously enjoying the view as she scrambled to get dressed. His dark eyebrows were raised even higher, an expression she was used to seeing when she told people what she did for a living. She was young to be where she was careerwise and being petite made her seem younger still.

"Not really. I just worked hard, like you. Then again, in my experience cardiologists are pretty impressed… with themselves." And was that an understatement, or what?

"I should be insulted, except it might be true." He grinned at her. "So what brings you to Paris?"

"Well, as I said, my work has to do with yours." And could there be a much worse situation? The very first time she had a one-time thing with a man, he turned out to be someone she'd be working with closely.

She still couldn't quite wrap her brain around this mess. With a nervous laugh threatening, she pulled on her shirt, relieved to be finally clothed. After all, being naked when they made their formal introductions would be all kinds of ridiculous, wouldn't it?

She smoothed down her clothes and took a deep breath as she turned to him.

"As you know, your company hired the designer of the first valve replacement catheter to come study and observe the trial of your new one. That designer would be me."

His mouth actually fell open as he stared at her. It seemed he shook his head slightly, and that jittery laugh finally burst out of her throat. Clearly, he was as shocked by this crazy coincidence as she was. Though maybe it wasn't so crazy or much of a coincidence—after all, the Crilex Corporation was putting them both up at the same hotel where they'd met.

"You can't be…Dr. Girard," he said, still wearing an expression of disbelief.

"I am. And I'm equally shocked that you're Dr. Dunbar." Awkwardly, she stuck out her hand. "Avery Marie Girard. Nice to meet you."

That slow, sexy smile she'd found all too attractive throughout the day slipped onto his face again before he laughed. He reached to shake her hand, holding onto it. "It's an honor, Dr. Girard. Obviously, I've read about all you've accomplished. Your designs for various medical devices. Studied them for more hours than I care to think about as I worked with engineers to design the one we'll be testing. I…can't believe that you're…her."

"Because I'm young?" Or more likely because he'd already seen her naked, but maybe she could pretend it hadn't happened. As though *that* was possible.

"Because you're beautiful. And fun. And spontaneous. With silky hair you don't wear in a bun and crazy, colorful clothes instead of drab gray. Rain boots with ducks instead of orthopedic shoes." His eyes crinkled at the corners. "I'm obviously guilty of thinking of a very stereotypical brainiac scientist, and those stereotypes don't include any of the things you are."

"Jack Dunbar!" She shook her head mockingly, having heard it all before. "You shouldn't admit any of that. The Society of Women Scientists will publicly flay you if you say that aloud. Maybe mount your head on an energy stick and parade the streets with it, denouncing stereotypes of all kinds."

"And I'd deserve it." The eyes that met hers were warm and admiring. That admiration would doubtless change into something else if he knew about her true role in his project. A slightly sick feeling seeped through her. Why, oh, why, hadn't she learned who he was before she'd slept with him?

"Glad you admit it. Scientists come in all ages, sizes, genders and personalities."

"You're right, and I'm sorry." He got out of the bed as well, and she averted her gaze from his glorious nakedness. "Sounds like you buy into some stereotyping, too, though. That cardiologists are all egotistical and impressed with themselves."

Guilty. But she had good reason to believe that, and it wasn't based on a stereotype. It was based on personal experience. And then, today, she'd dived into bed with another one. How stupid could she be? "Let's agree to set those preconceived ideas aside, shall we?"

"Agreed." He shook his head as he pulled on his own clothes. "Wow. I'm just blown away by this. I'd been interested in meeting the famous Dr. Girard and pleased to have her participate in the trial with me. Little did I know she'd be an incredible tour guide, have the greenest eyes I've ever seen and…" he paused to look at her, speaking in the low, deep rumble that did funny things to her insides "...the sweetest lips on either side of the Atlantic Ocean."

Oh, my. And his were beyond sweet, as well. "Except you realize this was a bad idea. Now that we know we'll be working together."

In fact, he didn't have any idea exactly how bad an idea it had been.

Robert Timkin, the Crilex CEO, had spun to Jack and everyone else involved that Avery would be there just to observe the trial for her own education. But the company knew she had concerns about the new device and had really hired her to evaluate the data, giving her the power to stop the rollout of the next trials if she thought it necessary.

Jack had worked on designing the new device and organizing the trial for over a year, and he'd doubtless flip out if the data forced her to shut it down.

"Working together." His warm smile faded and his brows lowered in a frown. "I guess you're right. That is a problem."

"It is." She drew a calming breath. "Listen. This afternoon was wonderful. A lovely day in a wonderful city between two strangers. But now we're not strangers. And I have to be an objective observer as I gather data on the trial. From now on, we're just working colleagues, nothing more."

He stared at her silently for a moment, his expression serious, before he nodded. "You're right. Business and pleasure never mix well."

"No. They don't." Not to mention that she'd sworn off cardiologists for good.

He stepped forward and pulled her close, pressing

his lips to hers in a soft, sweet kiss. Despite her words and thoughts and conviction, she found herself melting into him.

"That was from Jack to Avery. Thank you for an unforgettable day," he whispered against her lips before he stepped back. "Dr. Dunbar will be meeting Dr. Girard tomorrow in the cath lab as we both concentrate on why we came to Paris. Okay?"

"Okay."

He dropped one more lingering kiss on her mouth before he picked up her coat and draped it over her arm. She stepped out to the hall and the door clicked quietly behind her. She lifted her fingers to her lips, knowing with certainty this had been the only one-time fling she'd ever have. That she'd savor the memory, and pray that over the next thirty days it didn't come back to sting her in more ways than one.

CHAPTER THREE

AVERY STOOD BEHIND a wall of glass to one side of the operating table in the hospital's cath lab, watching the procedure on the X-ray fluoroscopy viewing monitor. She'd gowned and masked like everyone else in the room, but unlike anyone else, she held a tablet in her hand to record the notes she'd be taking.

"The prosthetic valve is made from cow tissue," Jack said to the nurses and doctors assisting or observing the procedure, as he and Jessica Bowman, the nurse he'd brought with him from the States, readied the patient. "This version doesn't require a balloon to open it as the previous one did."

He continued to explain, as he had last night during his presentation, how a transcatheter aortic valve implantation, TAVI, worked. The details of how the catheter was designed, and why the stent and valve were in an umbrella shape, designed to push the diseased valve aside before the umbrella opened, seating the new valve in its place. With the procedure not yet started, Avery had a moment to watch him instead.

Today, he was all business, his dark eyes serious above his mask, his voice professional and to the point. In stark contrast to yesterday's amusing and witty companion. As they'd laughed and walked through Paris, his eyes had been perpetually filled with interest and humor, his mouth curved in a smile, his attention on her as much as it had been on the landmarks she'd shown him.

A very dangerous combination, this Dr. Jack Dunbar. So dangerous she'd thrown caution off the top of the Eiffel Tower. Thank heavens they'd agreed that no more hot, knee-melting kisses or spontaneous sex could be allowed.

Though just thinking about those kisses and their all-too-delicious lovemaking made her mouth water for more.

She gave herself a little mental smack. Date a cardiologist? Been there, done that. Twice. Fool me once, shame on me, fool me twice, shame on me again. Fool me three times? Well, her genius status would clearly be in question.

Then there was the other sticky issue. Obviously, the best-case scenario would be for the device to work fabulously, for the trial to be a success and for it to be further rolled out to other countries and hospitals. After all, in the U.S. alone over one hundred thousand people each year were diagnosed with aortic stenosis, and a solid third of them were high risk who might not do well with traditional open-heart surgery or weren't candidates at all.

But, from studying this stent and catheter, she worried that it didn't fully address the significant problem of postoperative valve leakage and subsequent pulmonary edema, which her own design had not solved and was something she was trying to fix in her new prototypes.

"I'm going to establish a central venous line through the right internal jugular," Jack said as he made an incision in the patient's neck. "Then insert a temporary balloon-tip pacemaker. Both groin areas of the patient have been prepped, and I'll next insert an introducer sheath into the femoral artery."

Avery watched as his steady hands worked. After completing the first steps, he made another incision in the patient's groin, moving the guide wire inside the artery. "Contrast dye, please, and monitor the heparin drip," he said as he watched his maneuvering of the wires on the overhead screen. "You'll see that it's important to puncture the artery with a high degree of angulation to minimize the distance from the artery to the skin."

The man was an incredibly skilled interventional cardiologist, that was obvious. She quickly focused on the careful notes she was taking to squash thoughts of the man's many skills he'd thoroughly demonstrated to her yesterday. Why, oh, why, would she have to be around him every day when the whole reason she'd given in to temptation had been because she'd thought she'd never see him again?

Finally, he finished stitching the access sites and the patient had been moved to Recovery. Jack shook hands with all those in the room congratulating him.

"Thank you, but I'm just one cog in this wheel that will hopefully change valve transplantation forever," Jack said. "One important cog is right here with us. The designer of the first catheter-inserted replacement valve, Dr. Avery Girard."

Taken off guard, she felt herself blush as Jack turned, gesturing to her with his hand, then actually began to clap, a big smile on his face, as the others in the room joined him. She'd been keeping a low profile, and most of the hospital had just assumed she was a Crilex representative. Most cardiologists she knew—most definitely both of her old boyfriends—loved to play the big shot and preen at any and all accolades. Neither one of them would have shared the glory unless they had to.

"I appreciate your nice words, Dr. Dunbar," she said, feeling a silly little glow in her chest, despite herself. "I have every hope that the new design you've helped develop will be the one that works. Congratulations on your first procedure going smoothly."

"Thank you." His warm eyes met hers, reminding her of the way he'd looked at her yesterday, until the doctors observing converged on him to ask questions and he turned his attention to them.

Avery took off her gown, mask and hat, and caught herself watching Jack speak to everyone. Listening to his deep voice and the earnest enthusiasm there. She wanted to stay, to listen longer, but forced herself to move quietly from the room to go through her notes. Limiting her interactions with him to the bare minimum had to be the goal, and since there was just one surgery scheduled today, there was no reason to hang around.

Satisfied that her notes were all readable, in order and entered correctly into her database, Avery walked toward the hotel, feeling oddly restless. She'd planned to work in her room, but a peculiar sense of aloneness came over her. Since when had that ever happened?

Still, the feeling nagged at her, and she stopped to work for a bit at a little café, which seemed like a more appealing choice. After a few hours she headed to her room and settled into a comfy chair with her laptop.

Projects on her computer included ideas on how to fix her previous TAVI design if the one Jack had in trial had significant issues.

That unsettled feeling grew, sinking deep into the pit of her stomach, and she realized why.

If she had to recommend the trial be discontinued, would Jack think it was because she wanted Crilex to develop one of her designs instead? That her concerns would be from self-interest instead of concern for the patients?

She'd been doing freelance work ever since abruptly leaving the company that had funded her first TAVI design. They'd insisted on continuing the trials long after the data had been clear that the leakage problems had to be fixed first, which was why she'd been glad to observe this trial before that happened again.

If only she could talk to Jack about it, so he'd never think any of this was underhanded on her part. But her contract with Crilex stated she was to keep that information completely confidential.

She pressed her lips together and tried to concentrate on work. Worrying about the odd situation didn't solve anything and, after all, Jack knew she'd designed the original. Wouldn't he assume she was likely working on improvements to it and observing his with that in mind?

She couldn't tell Jack the power she had over the trial. But maybe she should tell him she had concerns with the design. To give him that heads-up, at least, and maybe nudge him to look for the same issues she would be as the trial continued.

Avery caught herself staring across the room for long minutes. With a sigh she shut the lid of her laptop and gave up. Clearly, she needed something to clear her head. Fresh air and maybe a visit to somewhere she hadn't been for a while. A place popped into her head, and she decided it was a sign that it might be just what she needed to get back on track.

A half hour later, jostling with others passengers as she stepped off the metro, she saw the sun was perilously low in the sky. She hadn't torn out the door in record time to miss seeing the Sacré Coeur at sunset and headed in that direction in a near jog, only to bump into the back of some guy who stepped right in front of her.

"Oh, sorry!" she said, steadying herself.

"No, my fault. I'm trying to figure out how to get to the Sacré Coeur to see it at sunset, and I…"

She froze and looked up as the man turned, knowing that, incredible and ridiculous as it was, the man speaking was none other than Jack Dunbar. Saw his eyes widen with the same surprise and disbelief until he laughed and shook his head. "Why is it that whenever I need a tour guide, the best one in Paris shows up to help me?"

Fate. It was clearly fate, and why did it keep throwing her and Jack together? Should she even admit that was exactly where she'd been going? "I wish I had the answers to the universe. But somehow I don't think you'll be surprised to learn that's where I'm headed, too."

He looked at her a long, serious moment before he gave her a slow smile, his eyes crinkling at the corners, and the warmth in them put a little flutter in her chest. "You know, somehow I'm not surprised. And who am I to argue with the universe? Guess this means we're going together."

A buoyant feeling replaced the odd, unsettled feeling she'd had for hours. Bad idea? Yes. Something she could walk away from? Apparently not.

"Then we've got to hurry." She grabbed his hand, knowing she was throwing caution away again. But how could she say no to the happy excitement bubbling up inside her? And after all, it was just a visit to the Sacré Coeur, right? "The sun's setting soon, and we don't want to miss it."

"Lead on, Ms. Tour Guide. For tonight I'm all yours."

CHAPTER FOUR

JACK LOOKED AT the adorable woman dragging him through the streets and wondered, not for the first time, how he could have gotten so lucky to have met her before they'd started working together. A personal connection before a professional one got in the way of it.

The professional part was unfortunate, since he'd vowed he'd never again get involved with a woman at work. For just one more night, though, he'd let himself enjoy being with Avery. After all, here they were, together. And, smart or not smart, he just couldn't resist.

"A lot of people think it's really old, but did you know the Sacré Coeur was consecrated after World War I in 1919?"

"I didn't know. Are you proving again to me that female scientists are well versed in many subjects?"

"I don't have to prove anything about women in science," she said in a dignified tone, "seeing as I'm not wearing orthopedic shoes."

He laughed. "True. And they're even bright green, which I've never seen in leather ankle boots."

"Clearly, you live a sheltered life. Maybe you should get yourself some brightly colored shoes."

"Somehow, I think my patients would worry about

my skills if I dressed that way." His eyes met her twin-kling ones, an even more vivid green than her boots, and just looking at her made him smile. "You get to hide in your lab and behind your computer. I don't."

"You could wear them while your patients are under anesthesia." She had that teasing look in her eyes that he'd found irresistible yesterday when they'd gone up the Eiffel Tower, then spent that magical time in his hotel room. That he'd found irresistible since the moment she'd grabbed his hand and led him to break-fast. That he had to somehow learn to resist, starting again tomorrow.

"Except most of my patients are awake during pro-cedures, so I'll stick with black or brown."

"Where's your sense of adventure?"

"Here with you tonight."

She looked up at him, an oddly arrested expression on her face. "Mine, too." She stepped up their pace. "We're almost there, and since January's off season, hopefully there won't be big crowds. Good thing the sun's peeking through. I think it just might be a beau-tiful night."

"It already is."

A blush filled her cheeks as she realized what he was saying. And maybe it sounded hokey, but he meant it. His intense focus on work usually didn't allow him to notice things like a beautiful sunset or, though he prob-ably shouldn't admit it, even a beautiful woman some-times. But she'd grabbed his attention from the second he'd met her, and he didn't know what to do about that.

She led him around a corner then suddenly stopped, turning her full attention in front of them. "*Voilà!* We made it! And, oh, my gosh, I think it's about the most spectacular I've ever seen!"

His gaze followed hers, and the sight was beyond anything he'd expected. At the end of the street behind a beautiful old building with large columns, the Sacré Coeur rose high above everything else. Its numerous cupolas and spires were bathed in pink and gold from the sunset, emerging from the pale sky and looking for all the world like a stunning mural in the mist.

"That's...incredible."

"It is, isn't it?" She took her hand from his, moving it to clutch his arm, holding him closer. He looked down to see her eyes lit with the same wonder he was feeling and that strange sense of connection with her, too, that had prompted yesterday's memorable interlude. "I haven't seen the basilica for a long time."

He moved his arm from her grasp and wrapped it around her shoulders, wanting to feel her next to him. They stood there together a long while, staring as the pastels changed hue and darkened. Eventually, the sun dipped low, taking the color and light with it, and Jack turned to her, pulling her fully into his arms without thinking. "Somehow, I don't think it would have seemed quite as beautiful if you hadn't been here with me."

She smiled and lowered her head to rest her cheek against his chest as she gazed down the street at the now shadowed church, and he couldn't believe how natural it felt to hold her like this. Like they'd been together a long time instead of one day. Like there weren't good reasons not to.

He stroked his hand up her back, sliding it beneath her thick hair to cup her neck. "How about we take the funicular up to see the city below?"

She lifted her head and leaned back to look up at him. "How do you know about the funicular?"

"What, you think you have all the dibs on tour guiding?" He tucked her hair under her cute hat, a yellow one this time, letting his fingers linger on the softness of her locks before stroking briefly down her cheeks. "I read a Paris tour guide book because I didn't know I'd have a personal one tonight."

"And yet here I am."

"Yeah. Here you are."

For a moment her green eyes stared into his until, to his surprise, worry and utter pleasure, she lifted herself up on tiptoe, slipped her arms up his chest and around his neck and pressed her lips to his. The touch was instantly electric, surging through every cell in Jack's body as he tightened his arms around her. Until he forgot they worked together. Until he forgot they were standing near any number of other sightseers who were snapping photos and admiring the church. On the side of a busy street where cars and motorcycles and scooters veered all too perilously close.

Just as had happened yesterday under that umbrella, Avery managed to make him forget everything but the drugging taste of her mouth as it moved softly on his.

The roar of a scooter zooming by had him breaking the kiss. He leaned his forehead against hers, their little panting breaths creating a mist of steam in the cold air between them. "Wow. That was nice."

"What, you think you have all the dibs on initiating a kiss?"

He chuckled at her words, mimicking his. "Believe me, I'm more than happy to share the dibs. But as much as I'd like to keep kissing you, I don't want either of us sent to the hospital by one of the crazy drivers around here." Or get into a sticky situation because of their jobs. "Let's go on up to see the view."

She pulled away and something, maybe embarrassment, flickered in her eyes. He reached for her chin and turned her face to his. "Hey, what's that look for?"

"I don't know why I kissed you. Why I keep kissing you, even when we agreed not to." She shook her head, a little frown between her brows. "It's like something comes over me and I lose all common sense."

"If you have to lose your common sense to kiss me, I hope you don't find it," he teased, earning a small smile. He took a few steps backward, bringing her with him, until he came up against the wall of a building. Even as he knew he shouldn't, he lifted his hand to cup her cheek, gently stroking her beautiful lips with his thumb. "You taste damned good to me."

"Except we need to work together. So kissing or… anything else…isn't a good idea."

"I know. It's a hell of a bad idea." He kissed her again, and the sigh that slipped from her lips, the way her body relaxed into his nearly had him going deeper, and to hell with the risk of being struck by a car. But he forced himself to let her go, reaching for her hand. "Come on. Your funicular awaits, princess."

They rode to the top and enjoyed the incredible views of the city as he held her close to shelter her from the colder air and wind. They meandered along the cobbled streets of Montmartre as Avery filled him in on some of the history of the village that had long been a haven for artists, including Picasso, Monet and Van Gogh. Today it attracted young artists who peddled their work on the streets.

"I don't know about you, but I haven't eaten," Jack said as they passed a restaurant with an appealing exterior. He looked at the posted menu and laughed when he realized it was, of course, in French. "I don't know what this place serves, but you want to grab something to eat?"

"My parents and I lived right here in Montmartre the two years we were in Paris, but I've never eaten here," she said, looking at the menu. "It's pretty expensive."

"We deserve something besides hospital food, which we'll be eating a lot of. Come on."

The food turned out to be good, and they enjoyed a lively conversation and occasional debate about medical devices like stents and implants until they both laughed about it.

Jack grabbed the bill when he saw her reaching for it, handing his credit card to the waiter. "My treat. I like a woman who eats all her food and talks about something besides shopping," he said to tease her.

"You treated me yesterday, so it should be my turn. And it sounds like you've been dating the wrong kind of women."

"No doubt about that." In fact, she didn't know how right she was, and it was a good reminder why he couldn't date Avery, no matter how attractive she was. No matter how much he wanted to.

"I don't always practically lick the plate, though," she said with a grin. "Thank you. The food was amazing, but you spent way too much."

"You forget I'm a rich, egotistical cardiologist. When I'm not working like crazy, I like to throw money around to impress beautiful women."

"You're right. Somehow I'd forgotten."

Her smile disappeared. He had no clue why and tried for a joke. "It's my pleasure to shower money on gorgeous scientists who wear colorful shoes."

Still no smile. In fact, an odd combination of unhappiness and irritation had replaced every bit of the pleasure that had been on her face.

Well, damn. But it was probably just as well, considering everything. "Time to head back to the hotel," he said, shoving back his chair to stand. "We have two surgeries tomorrow I need to get ready for."

She nodded and they headed toward the metro. It felt strange not reaching out to hold her hand, and a pang of regret filled him. But wishing their circumstance could be different didn't change a thing.

"Oh! I think that's Le Mur des Je T'aime! I've never seen it."

"What's Le Mur…whatever you said?"

He followed her as she moved closer to look at a wall of tiles with words scrawled all over it and splashes of red here and there in between. "It's the Wall of I Love You. An artist named Baron conceived of the wall, with 'I love you' written in something like three hundred languages. As a place for lovers to meet."

A place for lovers to meet? That bordered on overly sentimental as far as Jack was concerned. "Sounds like something from a chick flick, with a gooey happily-ever-after."

After he'd said it he thought maybe he should have kept his opinion to himself, and was relieved when she laughed. "Typical man. Not that I know much about lasting relationships and happily-ever-after."

"That makes two of us."

"Nobody you'd meet here at the wall? Old flame or old pain?"

"I've been too busy." The only woman who qualified as an "old pain" was the medical device sales rep he'd dated who, it had turned out, had used him big-time to advance her own career. He hadn't come close to being in love with her, but it had been damned embarrassing. Which was why he never dated anyone remotely connected to his work. And he needed to remember that.

She began walking toward the metro again, and they were mostly quiet on the way back to the hotel. Another sudden shower burst from the night sky that had them wet in an instant and nearly running the last blocks, intimately tucked beneath Avery's little umbrella.

Finally sheltered under the overhang in front of the hotel doors, she shook the rain from it. "Clearly, I'm going to need to get a bigger umbrella," she said, her voice a little breathless. "This one isn't nearly big enough for both of us."

Except, after tonight, they wouldn't be touring Paris together anymore. "I could invest in a big, yellow rain poncho and leave the umbrella to you. That would be pretty masculine and sexy, don't you think?"

"I don't know. People might mistake you for a giant lemon."

He loved her laugh and the way her eyes twinkled. Fortunately, other people loaded onto the elevator with them or he just might have found himself kissing that beautiful, smiling mouth of hers again. He grasped her elbow when they arrived on her floor and moved into the hall.

"What are you doing?" she asked. "You're staying on the eighteenth floor."

"I always walk a lady to her door."

"I don't think hotels count."

"Why not? There are so many doors in this huge place, you might get lost." He thought she'd smile at his teasing tone, but she didn't, and he sighed. "If that look on your face means you think I'm planning to jump your bones again, I'm not. Much as I'd like to, I get that it's different now. And agree it needs to be. Okay?"

"Okay."

She smiled, and it was her real, sunny smile. So real he had to kiss her one last time. She tasted the same as she had before, an intoxicatingly sensual mix of chilled, damp skin and warm mouth. The smell of rain and a slight, perfumed scent from her hair filled his nostrils, and the feel of her body through her coat filled his hands. He wanted to strip it off of her so that barrier wouldn't be between them.

A little sound came from her throat, and the sound inflamed him, his own low groan forming in response as he deepened the kiss. Damned if this woman didn't knock his socks off in every way a woman could.

She pulled back, her gloved hands a softly fuzzy caress on the sides of his neck. Her eyes were wide, her mouth wet from his kiss, her breathing choppy. "What is it about you?"

"Funny, I was just thinking the same thing. About you. Except I know the answer. You're amazing, and we have chemistry about equal to a nuclear explosion. Which makes it nearly impossible not to kiss you, even when I know I shouldn't." He pressed his lips to hers for another long moment before looking into the deep green of her eyes again.

She stared at him a moment longer before her beautiful mouth curved in an answering smile. "I guess we need to think of this as one last time Avery and Jack meet one another."

"I like that. A kiss dictated by the universe."

"By the universe." She rose up and kissed him again. Just as he was trying, in the midst of the thick fog in his brain, to mentally calculate how many hours it was until he had to be at work and alert, and how much longer he could enjoy the taste and feel of her, she drew back.

Her eyes were lit with the same desire he felt, and he was glad one of them had enough presence of mind to stop while they still could.

"There's something I want to be honest with you about," she said, clasping her hands together in an oddly nervous gesture. "And when you hear it, it'll probably help us keep our distance from one another."

"That sounds ominous. Is it that you're actually the one who's married?"

She smiled and shook her head. "No. It's about your TAVI device. I'm worried it doesn't address the flaw mine had. Leakage resulting in pulmonary edema."

He stared at her in surprise. "Why? We've barely begun the trial."

"I know. But I'm just not sure the corrections you've made will be enough, and feel it should have been tested longer on animals before a human trial."

What the hell? "The bioengineers and I worked hard to improve it. It's more than ready."

"I just wanted you to know I believe we should both pay extra attention to that aspect of the data."

Maybe this was how people felt when someone said their baby was ugly, and it wasn't a good feeling. "Duly noted. Good night, Dr. Girard."

He headed to his room, still reeling a little from her announcement. He was damned proud of the new device and would never have guessed she had any bias whatsoever about it. Surely she would remain scientifically impartial as she collected the data. Her announcement, though, did seem to make it easier to step away and keep his distance, which he tried to see as a positive development.

But as he attempted to sleep, he was surprised and none too happy to find himself thinking about Avery nearly as much as he was thinking of the work waiting for him early in the morning.

CHAPTER FIVE

JACK SAT AT the small desk the hospital had given him to use and finished his notes on the procedures they'd just completed. Now that surgery was over for the day, he let himself think about Avery and this uncomfortable situation.

For the first time in his entire career he'd had trouble getting one hundred percent of his focus on the patient and surgery in front of him before the procedure had begun. To not notice Avery standing behind the glass, ready to watch the TAVI procedure on the monitor, taking her notes. He'd finally managed, but somehow, some way, he had to keep Avery Girard and her premature concerns about the device from invading his thoughts.

He shoved himself from the chair to concentrate on what he'd come here to accomplish. He pulled up the patient records and headed toward the room of the second patient they'd done the procedure on.

Simon Bellamy was eighty-six years old and had been referred to them because of his severely diseased aortic valve. Although reasonably healthy otherwise, his age put him at high risk for open-heart surgery. He'd been doing well the past two days, and Jack expected he could be released tomorrow.

The satisfaction he was feeling as he looked at the patient's chart disappeared the instant he walked into the man's room.

Short, rasping gasps were coming from his open mouth, and he sat bolt upright in his bed, eyes wide. Jack grabbed his stethoscope from his scrubs pocket as he strode to the bedside. "What's wrong, Mr. Bellamy? Are you having trouble breathing?"

The patient just nodded in response, his chest heaving. Jack listened to the man's lungs, and the obvious crackling sounds were the last thing he wanted to hear. "Ah, hell." He pushed the button for the nurse, then got the blood-pressure cuff on the man. He stared at the reading, his chest tightening at the numbers. While it had been normal earlier today, it had soared to two hundred and twenty over one hundred.

The nurse hurried into the room. Jack kept his attention on his patient as he spoke, checking oxygen saturation levels, and was damned glad almost everyone in the hospital spoke English. "We need to reduce his heart's workload by getting his blood pressure down immediately. Also administer furosemide and get a Foley catheter placed, stat."

The man's oxygen level proved to be very low, which was no surprise. It was disturbingly obvious what was happening here. "I need to get a chest X-ray. Can you...?" He glanced at the nurse, who was busy getting the Foley placed. "Never mind. I'll call down to have the portable brought up."

And damned if the minute he finished the call to X-Ray, Avery walked in with her tablet in hand, stopping abruptly.

"What's wrong, Dr. Dunbar?"

For a split second he didn't want to tell her, after her revelation to him last night. Which would be childish and unprofessional, not to mention pointless, since she'd figure it out anyway. "Acute onset aortic insufficiency. Getting a chest film to confirm."

Just his luck that she was witnessing exactly what they'd just talked about. A significant complication from the valve leaking. He knew her being there or not didn't change the reality and told himself he was mature enough and confident enough to handle it. For a small number of patients it wasn't an unusual complication, anyway, and Jack discussed with everyone all the risks and potential side effects.

Avery gave a single nod and stepped out of the way as the tech rolled the X-ray machine into the room and got the patient prepared to get the picture of his lungs. To her credit, there was no sign of I-told-you-so smugness on her face, just concern.

"Have you given him a diuretic and blood-pressure meds?"

Had she really asked that? He nearly let loose on her, until he saw the deep frown over her green eyes and the genuine worry there. He managed to bite back the words he wanted to say, which was that he knew what he was doing, for God's sake, and to butt out. Did she really think he was a lousy doctor? "Having a Foley catheter placed and gave him furosemide and BP meds. With any luck, he'll be more comfortable shortly."

She nodded again, moving farther away to one side of the room as she opened her tablet. Her head tilted down and her silky hair swung to the sides of her cheeks as she began to tap away at the screen.

Frustration surged into his chest and he stuffed it

down, a little shocked at the intensity of it. His years of practicing medicine had taught him how to remain calm even in critical situations, and he was fairly legendary for being cool under fire.

He inhaled a deep, calming breath and turned away from her to check on Mr. Bellamy. Already the man was breathing a little easier and able to lean back against the raised bed. The X-ray tech ambled off with the films, and Jack hoped they'd be done fast, though he didn't expect them to show anything he didn't already know. There was no doubt in his mind this was pulmonary edema, the patient's lungs full of fluid from the valve leakage.

"Feeling slightly better now, Mr. Bellamy?"

The man nodded, still mouth-breathing but not nearly so labored as before. Jack reached for his hand and gave it a squeeze. "I know that's a scary thing, when you can't get a breath. You've been given a water pill to get your lungs clear, and we're going to keep the Foley catheter in to catch the fluid. It will have to stay there until we get the volume of fluid we want to see and make sure it's nice and clear. Okay?"

The man nodded again, giving his hand a return squeeze before Jack headed out of the room to check the X-ray.

"Dr. Dunbar."

Avery's voice stopped him in the hall and he turned. He folded his arms across his chest, wondering if this was the moment for an *I told you so*. Which he absolutely would react calmly and professionally to, damn it, if it killed him.

"Yes?"

She stepped close to him and, to his surprise, placed

her cool palm on his forearm. He couldn't figure out exactly what her expression was, but it didn't seem to be self-satisfaction. More like...remorse?

"I owe you an apology."

He raised his eyebrows. That was about the last thing he'd expected to come out of her mouth, and he waited to hear what she was apologizing for.

"It was completely inappropriate of me to ask if you'd administered blood-pressure meds and furose-mide. You're the doctor in charge and far more knowl-edgeable about patient care than I am."

"Yes, I am."

A little laugh left her lips. "There's that egotistical cardiologist finally coming out. I knew he was in there somewhere." She dropped her hand from his arm and gave him a rueful smile. "During the clinical trial on my original device, I was often required to give instruc-tions to nurses post-op when the doctors weren't around. I guess it's an old habit that's hard to break. Sorry."

She bit her lip, and damned if the thought of how in-credible it had been kissing her came to mind.

How could he be thinking about that now? He looked into the green of her eyes, filled with an obvious sincer-ity, and felt his frustration fade. "Just don't let it happen again, or everyone in the hospital might start to wonder if you know something they don't. Like that I bought my MD online."

"It would take more than me blurting something dumb to tarnish your awesome reputation, Dr. Dun-bar. Everyone here thinks you walk on water." Those pretty lips of hers curved. "But, believe me, I'll do my best to keep my trap shut. You know that old saying about how if looks could kill? Seeing the expression in your eyes at that moment, if that was true, I'd be lying on the floor lifeless."

In spite of everything, he felt himself smile, and how she managed that, he didn't know. "Cardiologists do have superpowers, you know. Better not test me to see if that's one of mine."

Her smile widened, touched her eyes and sent his own smile even wider. They stood looking at one another, standing there in the hallway, until Jack managed to shake off the trance she seemed to send him into with all too little effort.

He couldn't allow himself to fall any further for her obvious charms. Her work was too tangled up with his, and he'd promised himself never again.

He brought a cool, professional tone back to his voice. "I'm going to check on Mr. Bellamy's X-ray. I'll put the notes in his chart for your database."

He turned and strode down the hall, fighting a stupid urge to look over his shoulder to see if she was still standing there. When he stopped at the elevator he glanced back up the hall, despite his best intentions not to, and his heart kicked annoyingly when he saw her backside as she moved in the opposite direction. Riveted, he stared at the view. Her thick, shiny hair cascading down her back. That sexy sway of her hips, her gorgeous legs with their slender ankles, her delicate profile as she turned into a patient's room.

And found himself powerless against the potent memories of how she'd felt held close in his arms, the taste of her mouth on his, the feel of his body in hers.

Damn.

He focused on the gray elevator doors. This just might prove to be the longest month of his life.

CHAPTER SIX

"So, LADIES AND GENTLEMEN," Bob Timkin said, smiling at the group attending the late dinner meeting at the hotel, "we are encouraged at the success so far after a full week of the clinical trial. Patients and their families are pleased with the results, and I have great optimism as we look forward to the rest of the month."

The forty or so attendees clapped, a number of them turning their attention, smiles and applause toward Jack. He shifted slightly in his seat, wondering why it felt a little awkward. Not long ago he'd felt pleased with the media attention he'd gotten for his role in the development of the prototype device and the work involved in getting it finished and the trial set up. Happy that his mother, father and brother—all doctors—were proud of him and what he was trying to accomplish in memory of his granddad.

A large group effort had made it happen. The biomedical engineers had taken his suggestions to heart when they'd created the device. Crilex had funded it. French officials had seen the value of conducting the first trials here. He'd always been sure to include every one of them in his presentations and mention them in interviews.

But when it came down to it, the focus of others had been primarily on his work and his skills.

Avery's gaze met his across the room, and damned if he didn't have to admit she was probably why he felt this sudden discomfort. Her original design was the whole reason he had a new TAVI device at all. And while a slight valve leakage in a small percentage of patients was normal, he didn't like it that now three of the patients in this trial so far had experienced that complication. Statistically, that was far higher than the expected six percent, and that knowledge, along with Avery's announcement of her concerns, added to his unease.

He and Avery had managed to be simply cordial and professional to one another for the remainder of this first week. She also hadn't said anything to him about the latest patient with the valve leakage, which he'd been surprised but glad about. She must have finally seen it was still way too early to become truly concerned.

Jack nodded in acknowledgement of the recognition being sent his direction, but as his gaze again met Avery's he knew he couldn't stand her believing he was egotistical enough to think he alone merited the applause. Why what she thought of him mattered so much, though, wasn't something he wanted to analyze.

About to get to his feet and give a little speech about all the people deserving credit for the trial, Jack saw Bob moving from the lectern. Discomfort still nagged at him, but he figured it would be ineffective and even weird to start talking as the crowd began to stand and disperse.

Next thing he knew, he was looking at Avery again, and, disgusted with himself, quickly turned away. He would not allow himself to wonder what she was doing the rest of the evening. Would. Not.

He should go to his room and look over the history of the patient he'd be doing surgery on tomorrow. But an odd restlessness left him thinking he needed to do something else first, so he could concentrate later. Maybe a little downtime, listening to music in the lounge, would help him relax.

He moved toward the table where Jessica was sitting with some other nurses, yakking away like they'd become best friends. "Hey, Jess. How about a drink at the bar? We only have a single surgery tomorrow afternoon, so I think we can stay up one night past ten p.m."

"You don't have to ask me twice." She smiled at the women she was with. "Anybody want to join us?"

One by one they shook their heads. "I need to get home to get my little ones ready for bed," a young woman said. "Their papa will let them have crazy fun all night if I'm not there, then they will be tired and crying in the morning before school."

Another nodded in agreement, rolling her eyes. "*Oui.* My Raoul thinks that, if Maman's not home, dinner can be a chocolate croissant."

Jack smiled as everyone at the table laughed in agreement. It sounded just like his sister-in-law's gripes on the rare occasions his brother took over with the kids. If he was ever a dad, he'd try to remember this conversation and be more responsible.

That the random notion came to mind at all took him aback. Since when had he even thought about having a family? The answer was never. Work consumed his life.

For the first time, he wondered if that was all he wanted. If work could always be everything.

He shook his head, trying to shake off any and all peculiar and unwelcome notions. Paris was clearly doing strange things to him and had been since day one. He'd be glad when the month was over and the clinical trials continued elsewhere. Maybe he should consider talking to the Russian government about a winter trial in Siberia—if that didn't freeze some sense into him, nothing would.

He moved into the hotel lounge with Jessica, passing the dance floor as the heavy beat of music pulsed around them. "I can't believe I've worked with you for three years, but don't know your tipple," he said to Jess as they settled into a round, corner banquette.

"Like that's a surprise?" she said with a grin. "I don't think we've ever been out for a drink before. Ever. You're always still at work when I leave."

"We haven't?" He thought back and realized with surprise that was the case. "It bothers me to realize you're right. Though I'm pretty sure a big part of that was you falling for Brandon. And the two of you getting married thing was kind of a big deal."

"Okay, maybe that's true," Jess said, chuckling. "A cosmopolitan makes me pretty happy. Sounds extragood after the constant demands you've put on me this week."

"Cosmo it is."

He ordered from the waitress and was just about to ask Jess a few of the questions he realized he'd never bothered to ask her before when, out of the corner of his eye, he saw Avery walk into the lounge. Not alone.

Every ounce of the relaxation and good humor he'd managed to feel for the past five minutes died when he saw the guy who accompanied her.

Jack recognized him as a doctor from the hospital, though he didn't know him. A urologist, maybe. French. Well dressed, like most Parisians, and good looking to women, too, he supposed.

Jack watched the guy laugh at something she'd said. As she gifted him with her amazing smile in return, he pressed his palm to Avery's lower back and led her to the dance floor.

The way she moved, the way she smiled, the way she rested her hand on the man's shoulder made it hard for Jack to breathe, reminding him of the moment they'd first met. Every muscle in his body tightened at the way the guy was looking at her as they moved to the beat of the music. Like she was first on his list of desserts.

"Earth to Jack. Should I call the bomb squad before it goes off?"

Jessica's words managed to penetrate his intense focus on Avery and the guy, and he slowly turned to her. "What?"

"You look like you're about to explode. Which I don't think I've ever seen from you. Jealous a little?"

"Jealous? That's ridiculous."

"It may be ridiculous, but I hate to break it to you. It's all over your face."

Somehow he managed to control his accelerated breathing. To school his expression into something he hoped was neutral. "I don't date women I work with. You know that."

"Uh-huh. Except this one's making you rethink that, isn't she?" Jack hadn't even realized the waitress had brought their drinks until Jessica took a sip of hers, studying him over the rim of her glass. "Listen. I get it. She's smart and pretty and, other than me, you're alone here in France. But acting on your attraction to her? That's just trouble calling your name."

Trouble with a capital *T*. Unfortunately, he'd felt that trouble calling his name ever since he'd arrived in Paris. Trouble in the form of a small woman with soft skin, smiling eyes and a mouth that tasted like bright sunshine on a gray day.

Had she joked with the guy that she chose dance partners based on who would buy her a drink? The thought squeezed his chest so tight he had to force out his response to Jess.

"Since when are you my guardian angel? Believe me, I know all of that, and you don't have to worry. I'm keeping my distance." At least, he'd managed to for the past week or so.

"Guess you'd better run, then, because she's heading toward our table."

He stiffened and turned. Then couldn't help the relief he stupidly felt when Dr. Frenchman wasn't with her. And hoped like hell he wasn't looking at Avery the same way that guy still was, watching her from a corner table.

"Dr. Dunbar, may I speak with you for just a moment?" Avery asked when she stopped in front of them, her gaze flicking from him to Jessica and back.

He sat back, trying to pretend she didn't affect him in any way, which stretched his acting skills to the limit. "What's on your mind?"

She stood silently for a moment. Jack took in how perfectly the yellow shift dress she wore fit her slim body. How she folded one hand over the other in a nervous gesture before she stilled them against her sides. How her silky eyebrows twitched the way he'd noticed before when she pondered what to say.

"I wanted to suggest that, when you have a day off soon, you let me show you—"

As though pulled by a string from some invisible puppeteer, he reached out to grasp her wrist, tugging her down onto the bench seat. Her hip bumped into his as her eyes widened in surprise. Jessica's presence had nearly helped him resist the urge but, God help him, the hot jealousy that had grabbed him by the throat took control. Wanting to send a message to the guy still sitting across the room. Prompting Jack to say what he couldn't stop thinking about, and before he knew it the words were coming out of his mouth.

"Show me the correct way to use an umbrella?" Of its own accord, his voice went lower as he dipped his head, his lips nearly touching hers. "Or explain the mysteries of chemistry and spontaneous combustion? In which case, we can find a more private place to talk."

She stared at him, and even through the darkness of the bar he could see the surprise and confusion on her face. "Um, no. I wanted to talk to you about the trial."

"What about it?"

"With three patients already experiencing valve leakage, I'm sure you see why I'm concerned."

He watched her lips move, thinking about how good it was to kiss her. Let his gaze travel to the V of skin below her throat, which he knew was soft and warm. "The trial's barely started. We haven't had nearly enough patients to come to any kind of conclusions yet."

"I know. But as I said before, sometimes there are red flags right away." Deeply serious, her green eyes locked with his. "I want to introduce you to a patient who underwent one of the first TAVI procedures with my original device. I'd like you to see what he's living with."

He laughed, disgusted with himself. While he couldn't stop thinking about the taste of her mouth and the softness of her skin, she didn't seem to be having any trouble focusing on work.

He realized he was still holding onto her wrist, and dropped it. "I know what people with postoperative complications live with, Avery. I treat them every day."

"Just think about my offer." As she lifted her hand to his shoulder, a part of him liked having it there, while the saner part reminded him she'd just had that same hand on Dr. Frenchman's shoulder. "You might find it enlightening to meet this man and his family."

She slid from the seat and walked away. To Jack's surprise, she didn't sit with Dr. Frenchman. Instead, she exited the bar entirely, and he was glad he didn't have to watch her cozy up to the man, at the same time annoyed as hell that he felt that way.

What was it about this woman? First he'd grabbed her and pulled her down next to him like he had a right to. And in spite of it being a beyond-bad idea, every time he looked at her, all he could think of was how much he'd enjoyed being with her and kissing her and having sex with her. How much he wanted more of all of it.

"Boy, you've got it bad." Jessica shook her head. "I hope you can keep from getting so tangled up with her that you lose perspective on what we came here to do."

As he watched Avery's bright yellow, curvy behind disappear into the hotel foyer, he could only hope for the same thing.

CHAPTER SEVEN

AVERY STEPPED OFF the hotel elevator to head to the front doors, then stood frozen when she saw Jack standing right where she wanted to go. An absurdly handsome Jack, wearing a pale blue dress shirt, necktie and sport coat.

She and Jack had been friendly but professional over the past two days of surgeries and patient follow-ups, and she hoped it could stay that way. Without the uncomfortable attraction that remained in a low hum between them. The attraction that had clearly prompted Jack to do the caveman thing and pull her down next to him after she'd danced with the French doc she'd met. Jessica was walking toward him, and Jack's mouth tipped into a smile when he spotted her. Normally wearing scrubs all day, Jessica had dressed up tonight, looking very attractive in a black dress with a coat slung over her arm. Obviously, the two were going to dinner somewhere, and when Jessica reached Jack she said something that made him laugh.

Could there be something going on between them, now that she and Jack had agreed to keep their professional distance?

The thought twisted her stomach in a strange little

knot, which was ridiculous. Must be just a residual re-action to the shock of her ex cheating on her.

Still, the thought of walking past Jack and Jessica to leave the hotel made her feel uncomfortable, though that wasn't very mature. Hoping they'd move on to wherever they were going, she saw Jack pull his phone from his pocket. In just seconds his expression went from relaxed to a deep frown, and the sudden tension in his posture was clear even from all the way across the room.

Jack shoved his phone back into his pocket, spoke briefly to Jessica, and pushed open the doors to head out into the night. Was there a problem with a patient? Without thinking, Avery hurried to talk to Jessica, to see if there was anything she could help with.

"Jessica?"

The woman turned, and when she saw Avery the concern on her face morphed into a neutral expression. "Yes?"

"I couldn't help but notice that Jack ran out of here quickly. Is something wrong?"

Jessica seemed to study her before she answered. "One of the patients we performed surgery on today is experiencing slurred speech and weakness in one arm."

Obviously, a possible stroke. "Which patient?"

"Henri Arnoult."

"All right. Thanks." Avery took a step toward the doors to head over there, but Jessica's hand on her arm stopped her.

"There's nothing you can do, Dr. Girard. He'll either make it or he won't, and you know as well as I do that stroke is one of the major risks of any kind of surgery involving stents."

"I do know. But it's my job to record every bit of data

on every patient, whether it's a normal complication or not, and whether it's a good outcome or a bad one."

"Jack told me you have some concerns about this TAVI device. I hope your personal bias wouldn't interfere with—or influence—that data."

"I don't have any personal bias. Concerns, yes. Bias, no." Jessica regarded her with clear skepticism, and Avery sighed. "Listen. I appreciate that you support Jack, and I assure you that any and all data I record and analyze will be done carefully and scientifically. I'd love for this trial to be a success as much as you do."

"Good. Jack is the best surgeon I've ever worked with, and this groundbreaking work is extremely important to him. Important to heart patients, too."

"I know."

"Okay," Jessica said, nodding. "Please ask Jack to let me know how things go. Even if it's in the middle of the night."

"I will." As soon as Avery pushed open the door, cold wind whipped down her neck and up her dress. She closed her coat as tightly as she could and hurried the two blocks to the hospital.

She found Jack in the patient's room in the ICU, talking to the house doctor who had likely been the one to call him in. Avery hung back, not wanting to intrude inappropriately. It seemed like forever before the house doctor finally left the room. Avery inhaled a fortifying breath before she entered. Jack stood there, his back to the door, his hands in his pockets, looking down at the patient lying in the bed. She moved to stand beside him, her heart sinking when she saw that Mr. Arnoult was unconscious and connected to a breathing machine.

Without thinking, she tucked her hand through the

crook of Jack's arm and his elbow, pressing it close against his side. "These are the tough days, I know, Jack," she said softly. "Do you know what's wrong?"

"He seemed fine when I saw him this afternoon. But I'm told his blood pressure soared and his speech became slurred, so they quickly got a CAT scan. Which confirmed he's had a large hemorrhagic stroke."

"It's not impossible that his condition could improve."

"No. Not impossible. We've given him meds to try to control the brain swelling, among other things, but I don't know. It's a big bleed."

"Have you…checked to see how the TAVI looks? Is it still in place?"

"Not yet. I just ordered an echocardiogram. I hope to God it hasn't moved, because there's no way he could survive open-heart surgery on top of this. Hell, he wouldn't have survived that kind of surgery before this." A deep sigh lifted his chest. "I suppose this is more confirmation to you that the trial might be premature."

He turned to look at her as he spoke, his eyes somber with concern. Her heart filled with the certain knowledge that it was for this ill man and not concern for himself or for the future of the trial.

"Will it shock you when I say no?" She pulled her hand from his arm to rest it against his cheek. "Risk of stroke is an unfortunate complication of any procedure like this. Give an elderly patient with serious underlying health problems the blood thinners necessary for this kind of surgery, and sometimes it doesn't go the way everyone hopes it will. It's no one's fault. It's not your fault or the device's fault. It just is."

He stared down at her for a suspended moment before, to her surprise, he gathered her in his arms. Another deep sigh feathered across her forehead as he rested his head on top of hers. She pushed aside his necktie before pressing her cheek against his chest, and she wrapped her arms around him, too, since he clearly needed that connection right now. He smelled wonderful, just as he had on their first day together, holding her close beneath that umbrella, and she found herself closing her eyes at the pleasure of it as she breathed him in.

"I'd hoped we wouldn't have any catastrophic events," he said as his hand stroked slowly up and down her back. "But you're right. It is a reality that this happens sometimes. And I appreciate you not making it even worse by stomping up and down and yelling about it."

"Wow. Sounds like you think I'm a troll or something."

"A troll?" She could hear the smile in his voice. "That, I've gotta say, never occurred to me."

It took great force of will for Avery to lean back and break the close contact between them. She glanced at Mr. Arnoult and the steadily beeping monitors and figured they should continue their conversation elsewhere.

"I could use some coffee. You?"

At his nod, she took his hand and they walked to the nearly empty coffee shop on the first floor. Sitting at a round table so tiny their knees kept bumping, Avery sipped her espresso before asking the question she needed to know the answer to. "Jessica seemed to think I might skew the data based on what she called my bias about the device. Do you, too?"

"Honestly?" He quirked a dark eyebrow. "I'd be lying if I said it hadn't crossed my mind."

Her chest ached a little at his words. Obviously, there'd be no friendship between them if that was how he felt. And she realized, without a doubt, that she very much wanted that friendship. More than friendship, but under the circumstances friendship was all they could have.

And even friendship was probably a bad idea, considering Jack didn't know all that Crilex had hired her to do.

"I find, though, that for some damned reason," he continued as he leaned closer, his mouth only inches from hers, "the uncertainty seems to turn me on."

A startled laugh left her lips. "And my wondering if you're different or the same as most other cardiologists apparently has kept me interested, as well."

He leaned closer still, so close his nose nearly touched hers. "Or maybe it's that we just have this undeniable chemistry that refuses to be snuffed out by little things like that."

The timbre of his voice, the expression in his dark eyes made her a little breathless. "Well, I did get straight As in chemistry. It's something I'm good at."

"Now, that I already knew." He closed the tiny gap between them and gave her the softest of kisses. "I'm going to go check on Mr. Arnoult again and see if the echocardiogram's been done. You might as well go on back to the hotel, or wherever you were going to go tonight, and collect his data tomorrow. Unless your plan was to go out with Dr. Frenchman. He's a total player, and even more egotistical than I am."

"You mean the man I danced with?" Was it wrong

of her to be pleased at the tinge of jealousy in his voice, to know that he'd noticed and had obviously been bothered by it? Was it also wrong of her that she'd secretly hoped he would, even though she'd been disgusted with herself when the thought had occurred to her? "I didn't realize you knew him."

"I don't. I just know his kind."

"Uh-huh. Aren't you the man who told me I shouldn't judge you negatively just because of what you do for a living?"

"That's totally different. Trust me, I know how guys think and saw the way he was looking at you."

"What way?"

"Like I do." She'd never known something like a hot twinkle existed, but there it was in his eyes as he stood. "I'm going to spend the night here so I can keep tabs on Mr. Arnoult."

A sudden desire to stay right here with him, supporting him, came over her, but she knew it didn't make a lot of sense. She wasn't Mr. Arnoult's family, she wasn't a medical doctor, and she and Jack needed to keep a professional distance. Though, at that moment, as her gaze stayed connected with his, she knew with certainty that was getting more difficult every day.

Concern for Mr. Arnoult and thoughts of Jack staying up much of the night, working, left Avery unable to sleep well, either. Up early and in the hospital just after 7:00 a.m., she stopped in the hospital coffee shop to get double shots of espresso for both her and Jack, knowing she'd find him there somewhere.

She checked Mr. Arnoult's room first, relieved to see Jack was there, able to drink his coffee while it was still somewhat hot. Her heart squeezed the second she saw him standing next to the patient's bed, his dark head tipped toward the nurse and another doctor as he spoke to them.

Mr. Arnoult was still connected to the ventilator, and from her distance by the door it appeared he was still unconscious or heavily sedated. The squeeze in her chest tightened when she saw his head was thickly bandaged, which most likely meant they'd decided to try draining the hemorrhaging blood from around his brain.

Jack glanced up as she entered the room, and his gaze held hers for a moment before he finished his conversation and walked to meet her in the doorway.

"I could smell that coffee all the way across the room," he said. His hair was uncharacteristically messy, dark stubble covered his cheeks, and the lines at the corners of his eyes were more pronounced. "Nothing better than a woman who understands a caffeine addiction."

"I nearly got you a triple, but thought maybe I could get you to go to the coffee shop I took you to that first day. It would be good for you to get out of the hospital for a breath of air."

He shook his head. "Not yet. Maybe later."

"How is he?"

He grasped her elbow and led her down the hall to the little office he'd been working from, pulling the single chair from behind the desk for her to sit on.

"No, you sit," she said, perching on the side of the desk. "You're the one who's been up most of the night."

"If I sit, I might fall asleep." He set down his coffee, giving her a shadow of a smile as he took hold of both her shoulders and gently lowered her into the chair. "A woman who brings coffee deserves not only the chair but being draped in gold, like you said women should be."

"Well, coffee is worth its weight in gold." She sipped her espresso and resisted the urge to ask again about Mr. Arnoult. Forced herself to be patient and wait for him to speak when he was ready.

With his body propped against the side of the desk and long legs stretched out, he drank his coffee and stared out the door. Just when she thought she couldn't keep silent another second, he put his cup down and turned to her. "Things aren't good. We couldn't control his brain swelling, so the neurosurgeon drained the blood from his brain about two this morning. I had hoped that releasing the pressure would work, but the swelling continued. Tests show there's now severe, irreversible brain damage—his pupils are fixed and dilated. No movement of his extremities, no gag reflex. Just received CAT scan images that confirm it. Which I'm going to have to share with the family when they get here."

"I'm so sorry, Jack." She stood and moved in front of him to hold both his hands in hers. "I know this is never the outcome anyone wants. But as I said yesterday, we both know this risk exists in a patient like him. He was extremely ill before the procedure. You'd hoped to give him a new lease on life, which he had no chance of having without replacing his valve, and he wouldn't have made it through open-heart surgery for that. You tried your best."

He released her hands, his tired eyes meeting hers. "Thanks for all that. I do appreciate it. I know it, but it still feels crappy."

Without thinking, she slipped her hands around his neck and kissed him. Just like she had in front of the Sacré Coeur. This time, it was to comfort him, soothe him. But the moment her lips touched his, the moment his arms wrapped around her and held her close, the moment his warm, soft mouth moved against hers she nearly forgot the goal was comfort and not something entirely different.

But they were in an office attached to a busy corridor, which both of them seemed to remember at the same time. Their lips separated, and she rested her head on his shoulder as she hugged him, working on the comfort part again, stuffing down the other feelings that wanted to erupt.

It felt good to hold him. Felt good to try to offer him comfort. But as the moment grew longer, warmer, she reminded herself that she was there for another reason, too. She should ask him about the prosthetic valve and if he'd checked it or not, but she didn't want to break the closeness they were sharing. Not quite yet, anyway. The valve wasn't the reason the man had had the original stroke, and she'd find out soon enough if it had moved or leaked after the brain had begun to bleed.

Apparently, though, this connection between her and Jack seemed to include mind reading. "I already know you well enough to guess you're dying to know about the valve," he said, loosening his hold on her to lean back. "We've done two separate Doppler echocardiograms, neither of which showed any fluid flow around it. It's fitting tight as a drum, which makes me all the sadder that he stroked before he could enjoy his life a little more."

She nodded. "That's encouraging for other patients

but, yes, it's very sad for Mr. Arnoult. Would you like for me to join you when you talk to the family?"

"No. This is a part of what I do. The hardest part, but the buck has to stop with me."

She nodded again, and instantly pictured the caring and sympathy that Jack would show the man's family when he shared the bad news, because it was obvious that was simply a part of who he was.

"Then I'll leave you. How about letting me give you a little TLC later? I'm good at that." As soon as the words came out of her mouth and a touch of humor lit his eyes, she knew how he'd interpreted it. And found her heart fluttering, even though that wasn't how she'd meant it.

"I bet you are. And despite us agreeing we shouldn't mix business with pleasure, I can't seem to keep all that in the forefront of my mind when you're around." He tipped up her chin. "Something else seems to take over instead. Like serious anticipation of some TLC from you."

He gave her a glimmer of a smile, his dark eyes connecting with hers for a long, arrested moment. Then he kissed her in the sweetest of touches. The rasp of his beard gently abraded her skin, and he tasted of coffee and of deliciousness, and she could have kept on kissing him for a long, long time. But his lips left hers to track, feather-light, up her cheek and linger on her forehead before he drew back. "Thanks for being here. I'll find you later, okay? Maybe dinner?"

She'd barely had time to respond before he left the room, his posture proud and erect despite the exhaustion he had to be feeling. And at that moment she knew with certainty that Jack was nothing like her old boyfriends. He had an integrity and warmth and depth they couldn't even begin to match.

Avery concentrated on seeing all the patients who were still in the hospital after their procedures, carefully recording their vitals, test results, state of mind and comfort levels. But throughout those hours she often found herself thinking of Jack having to continue on and do his job. How he'd still operated on the patient scheduled for early that morning, his focus never wavering throughout the procedure as she'd watched, despite the obvious fatigue in his eyes.

She'd bumped into him once, rounding on patients, spending a long time talking with each of them, recording his own notes. She wondered if he'd spoken with Mr. Arnoult's family yet, and her chest tightened at how tough that was going to be on all of them.

As she moved down the hall to see a different patient, she heard the rumble of his voice in Mr. Arnoult's room and the sound of quiet weeping. Her stomach clenched, and when she glanced in she saw two middle-aged men standing, flanking an elderly woman who sat in a chair, dabbing her face with a crumpled tissue. Jack was crouched in front of her, one hand patting her shoulder, the other giving her another tissue he'd pulled from the box on a chair next to her.

Avery found herself pressing her hands to her tight chest at the sweet and gentle way Jack was talking with the woman, the deeply caring expression on his face. A part of her wanted to go into the room and stand next to him for support, but she knew he wouldn't want or need that. It wasn't her place to spy or eavesdrop, ei-

ther, and she quickly moved on to the last patient she
needed to see.

At that moment, she knew she wanted to somehow
help him feel better about it all. While she knew this
was far from the first time in his career he'd had to de-
liver bad news to a family, and certainly wouldn't be
the last, giving him a reason to smile suddenly became
her priority for the day.

How, though? They'd already been up the Eiffel
Tower and seen the Sacré Coeur at sunset. Her mind
spun through her favorite places in Paris, but many of
them were more fun to go to in the summertime, when
you were lucky enough to enjoy some sunshine and
the gardens were glorious. Still, there was something
to be said for just walking the city on a cold night, cuddling to stay warm on a bench in one of the gardens or
by the Seine.

Cuddling? Her plan for the evening was about cheer-
ing Jack up, not kissing him or having sex or anything
like that.

Except she'd be lying to herself if she pretended that
she hadn't thought about throwing aside the very good
reasons they shouldn't be together for one more memorable night. A night to help him forget a very long and
difficult day. Knowing it would be more than memorable for her, too, would be the icing on the cake.

CHAPTER EIGHT

AVERY'S HEART, WHICH only moments ago had felt all bubbly at the thought of spending the evening with Jack and finding ways to make him happy, stuttered, then ground to a halt.

Standing stock still now just outside the doorway to Jack's office, she stared at what seemed like a reenactment of her warm and intimate time in that room with him earlier. A woman had her arms wrapped around his waist, and he held her close with his cheek resting on her head.

But unless Avery was watching some holographic image of that moment in time, Jack was not holding her. He was holding a different woman.

Jessica.

Barely able to breathe, Avery backed up a few steps, then turned to hightail it out of there.

She'd become completely, utterly convinced he wasn't at all like the last two doctors she'd been involved with, which proved how incredibly bad she must be at judging character. Clearly, every one of them charmed, lied and cheated as easily as they breathed, and she thrashed herself for forgetting. For thinking Jack was different.

She stalked down the hall, her throat tight with embarrassment as she thought of the really good fantasies
she'd been dreaming up about their night together. Gull-
ible idiot. Fool. IQ genius with no brains.

"Avery." Jack's voice and footsteps followed her, and
she walked faster. "Avery, stop, damn it!"

His fingers curled around her arm, turning her toward him. She yanked her arm from his hold. "What is
it, Dr. Dunbar? It's been a long day, and I have a date."
A date with herself and her computer and her work,
which she'd just remembered she'd promised herself
would be her only focus until she'd let a certain man
change her mind about that.

"Your date is with me. And if you're running off in a
huff because I was hugging Jessica, you know damned
well that she's married."

"Like that matters to some people."

"It matters to me. And to her. We've worked together
for three years. She's my coworker and my friend. And
as my friend, she felt bad about Henri Arnoult. Just
like you did. That's all." He grasped both her arms this
time, tugging her closer. "It's been a hell of a bad day.
Mr. Arnoult's family had to make the hard decision to
take him off the ventilator. We had to let him go. And,
yeah, that's one damned difficult part of being a doctor,
and I'm tired inside and out. The last thing I want is for
you to be upset and thinking things that are all wrong."

She stared into his dark eyes, which were filled with
frustration and exhaustion and worry. Could she have
been wrong? Jumped to conclusions too fast? And
hadn't she wanted to comfort him, not add to his stress,
if she was wrong?

She definitely didn't want to make his day any worse

than it already had been. But her heart didn't feel up to being exposed to more punishment, either. "Listen. I think it's a good idea for you and Jessica to be together tonight. She knows you better than I do, and you'll have a nice time, I'm sure."

"Except that, even though I shouldn't, I want to know you better." He glanced down the hall, which was fairly quiet this late in the day, before turning back again, lifting his hands to cup her cheeks. "After the great time we've spent together, how could you even think I might have something going on with Jess?"

She stared up into his eyes and could see he really wanted to know. But she didn't feel like sharing her past. Her embarrassment that she hadn't seen her exes for who they were.

"I didn't. Not really. I was just being weird."

His eyes crinkled at the corners in a smile. "The only way you're remotely weird is the odd color combinations you sometimes favor." His thumb stroked along her cheekbone before he bent his head and kissed her. Maybe it was stupid, but the soft warmth of his lips managed to sap every ounce of the worry and self-deprecation she'd felt just moments ago. The feel of his mouth slowly moving on hers sent all of that to the outer reaches of her brain and her thoughts back to the fantasies she'd been having before she'd seen him with Jessica and freaked.

He broke the kiss, and the eyes that met hers were so sincere she knew she couldn't let what had happened with her stupid exes mess with her mind anymore. No way did she want to live her life suspicious of people and their possible agendas, backing away from potential pain instead of exploring all the wonderful things the world had to offer.

That Jack just might have to offer, if their potentially disastrous professional relationship didn't ruin everything before they had a chance to spend more time together.

"It would sure be nice to kiss you without knowing there are hundreds of people who might be spying on us at any moment. Which is pretty much the only times we've kissed so far. Let's get out of here."

She wanted that, too, but felt she had to ask about Jessica's plans. After all, the woman probably had nothing to do, and maybe she shouldn't hog Jack all to herself. Even though that was all she wanted, darn it. "Shouldn't we ask Jessica to join us for dinner?"

"One of the reasons she was happy to come and assist me in the trial here is because she has a cousin with three little kids living in Paris. She's enjoying spending time with them. And even if she wasn't," he added, his eyes gleaming, "I wouldn't ask her along. Three's a crowd, and you're the one who said you're good at TLC and offered to comfort me, right?"

"I did make that offer, though you probably don't need it. You're pretty tough, I know."

"Tough or not, a guy always appreciates some TLC from a beautiful woman. Looking forward to being with you tonight is the only thing that made today bearable." He placed his mouth close to her ear, and his words, the rumble in his voice, made her shiver. "I know you don't back out on your promises. And I can't wait to be on the receiving end of some tender, loving care from the talented Dr. Girard."

* * *

Chilly wind nipped what little skin they had exposed, and Jack watched Avery tug her blue and purple scarf more tightly around her neck. Figured it was the perfect excuse to hold her even closer to his side as they walked through the Palais-Royal gardens. Though gardens would be an overstatement at the moment, since everything was dormant from winter, and the only things remotely green were the carefully trimmed evergreen shrubs.

"I love this park in the summertime, when all the roses are in bloom and you can sit and enjoy the quiet and seclusion from the busyness of the city," Avery said, smiling at him, her cute nose very pink from the cold. "And the trees are trimmed in an arching canopy that's fun to walk beneath on the way to the fountain. I'm sorry it's not all that pretty right now."

"You're sorry because you could do something about it being the end of January? Are you a magician as well as a scientist?"

"Wouldn't that be nice?" She laughed. "Sadly, no. I just wish I could show you the Paris I love all year round, but we'll have to settle for now."

Her words struck him with a surprising thought, which was that he wished for that, too. For more than just these brief weeks with her. But that wasn't meant to be. He had his work and his TAVI trials, which would take him to various parts of the world, and finally, assuming all went well, to trials back in the States. He didn't have time in his life for any kind of real relationship and felt a pang of regret about that reality.

"I'm enjoying the now with you," he said. "What's the next part of now, Ms. Tour Guide?"

"Let's pop into a few of these boutiques. Anything in particular you like to look at? Or want to buy?"

"Yes. The one thing I particularly like to look at is you." Which had been true from the moment he'd met her. He tugged her close enough that her steamy breath mingled in the cold air with his own. "And I'd like to buy a thin gold chain to slip around your neck, except you'd accuse me of being an egotistical player again. When the only reason would be to please you. Okay, and touch your skin, too. I'm definitely looking for ways to make that happen."

She blushed cutely, and he loved the humor that shone in her green eyes. "You don't have to buy me gifts to make that happen."

Maybe she saw exactly where his thoughts had immediately gone, because she stepped out of his hold to walk through the doorway of a little shop.

"In truth, I'm into this kind of thing more than gold," she said as she picked up a delicate, inlaid wooden box.

"Music boxes? Any special kind?"

"I love old ones. But any kind makes me smile. Like lots of little girls, I had one with a dancing ballerina and fell in love with them after that." She opened the lid and a tune began to play. An adorable smile lit her face and eyes, making him smile, too. "Isn't it beautiful?"

"Beautiful." He damned near took it from her hand to buy it for her, but was sure she'd protest. It would probably make her feel uncomfortable to receive a gift from him at that point in their relationship—or whatever you'd call the powerful force that kept drawing him to her.

They stared at one another, and the hum in the air between them was so strong it nearly drowned out the soft tune tinkling between them. She put the box down and, to his surprise, grabbed his hand and trotted quickly out of the store, the sexy blue ankle boots she wore clicking on the pavement.

"Where to now?" he asked.

"I just thought of something that would be fun to do with you."

He hoped that "something" was her hauling him off to the hotel to get naked for the TLC she'd promised, but had a feeling that was wishful thinking. "And that would be?"

"This." They ran until they got to a carousel, the music filling the air around it not all that different from the music box, except a lot louder. She jumped onto its platform, turning to him with the bright eyes and brilliant smile he'd come to see in his dreams. "Come on! Which horse do you want?"

"Whichever you're on."

She laughed and walked between the rows of wooden animals, finally straddling a white horse with a bright green saddle and carved mane that looked to be flying in the wind. Jack swung himself up behind her. As her rear pressed against his groin, as he wrapped one arm around her waist and one hand on top of hers on the pole, as he breathed in the scent of her hair and her skin, he knew he'd never see another carousel without remembering this moment with her.

"I never knew I loved merry-go-rounds until this moment," he murmured in her ear.

"Doesn't everybody?"

"Everybody lucky enough to have a gorgeous woman sharing their horse."

The music grew louder, and as the carousel began

to turn, their horse rose and fell, pushing his body into hers, rubbing them together. And damned if even through their clothes and jackets it wasn't just about the most erotic thing he'd ever experienced outside a bedroom.

He tried to scoot back, away from her a little, so she wouldn't feel exactly how aroused he was, but had a feeling she already knew. He dipped his head and let his lips wander over what skin he could reach, which wasn't nearly enough. Her cheek and jaw, her nose, her eyebrow. Her soft hair tickled his face as he nibbled her earlobe, tracing the shell of her ear with his tongue until her sexy gasp, the shiver of her skin he could feel against his lips, took every molecule of air from his lungs and sent him on a quest for her mouth.

The arm he had wrapped around her tightened as he lifted his hand from the pole to grasp her chin in his fingers, turning her face so he could taste her lips. Her eyes met his, a dark moss green now, full of the same desire he knew she could see in his.

Her head tipped back against his collarbone, and he covered her mouth with his and kissed her. Kissed her until he wasn't sure if the spinning sensation he felt was from the earth turning, the carousel revolving, the horse rising and falling or his brain reeling from Avery overload.

The sound of people laughing and talking seeped into his lust-fogged brain, and apparently Avery's, too, as they both slowly broke the kiss, staring at one another, the panting breaths between them now so steamy he could barely see her moist, still-parted lips. He brushed his thumb against her lush lower lip, and it was all he could do not to kiss her again.

"Didn't I say I'd like to kiss you, just once, without people standing around, watching?" he said when he was able to talk. "I don't think this accomplishes that."

She gave him a breathy laugh. "No. So let's accomplish it now."

As the carousel slowed to a stop, he slid from the horse, then helped her down. "Any ideas on how?"

"Oh, yeah." Her lips curved, and the only word to describe her expression would be *sensual*, which kicked his pulse into an even faster rhythm than it was already galloping in. "They don't call me the 'idea gal' for nothing."

CHAPTER NINE

JUST LIKE THE first time—the one she'd been sure would be the only time—Jack had her coat and blouse off before she'd barely drawn a breath. Time to get with the program and get his coat off, too. Her fingers weren't quite as swift as his talented surgeon ones, and she wrestled to get it unbuttoned.

He shrugged it off and tossed it on top of hers before reaching to touch his thumb to the top of her bra as he had before, slowly tracing the curve of it, and her breath backed up in her lungs at the expression in his eyes, at the low, rough sound of his voice. "Bright blue lace this time. Hard to decide if I like this or your pretty white one better."

"I have matching panties on. Does that help?"

His eyes gleamed in response. "Don't care if they match. I can't wait to see you in them." He lowered his mouth to hers, softly, sweetly, before moving it across her jaw, down to her collar bone, slipping farther until his tongue traced the lacy top of her bra. Sliding down to gently suck her nipple through the silky fabric until her knees wobbled. Avery clutched the front of his shirt, hanging on tight, wondering if she just might faint from lack of oxygen and the excruciating pleasure of it all.

She wanted to see his skin, too. Wanted to touch him and lick him, as well. "No fair that you're ahead of me," she managed to say, reaching for the buttons of his shirt. "No more distractions until I get your shirt off."

He lifted his head, ending his damp exploration of her bra, and his dark eyes gleamed into hers as she attempted to wrangle his buttons. "Happy to assist, if you'd like."

Oh, yes. She'd like. Mesmerized, she stared as he flicked open one button at a time, slowly exposing the fine, dark hair on his smooth skin, before finally pulling the shirt off entirely. About to reach for him, she lifted her gaze to his. Saw that his focus was on her breasts, and the hunger in his eyes sent her heart pounding even harder.

"You have one beautiful body, Dr. Girard."

"Funny, I was just thinking the same about you, Dr. Dunbar."

With a smile, he closed the gap between them, reached behind her, and in one quick motion had her bra unhooked, off her arms and onto the floor. His hand cupped her breast and his thumb moved slowly back and forth across her nipple until her knees nearly buckled.

"As I said before, those are some quick fingers you have, Dr. Dunbar. Should have known you were a surgeon or guitarist or something." She pressed her palms to his hard chest, sliding them through the dark, soft hair covering it. On up to wrap her arms behind his neck, holding him close, loving the feel of his body against hers as she moved backward, bringing him with her.

"You haven't seen anything yet," he said in a gruff voice so full of promise she found herself mindlessly touching her tongue to his jaw to taste him as she pressed her body to his. His mouth moved to capture hers as they continued their slow meander to the bed. She didn't even realize he'd unbuttoned her pants, too, until she felt his hands moving on her bottom, inside her silky underwear and on down her thighs until every scrap of clothing was pooled at her feet.

She gasped in surprise, which sent the kiss deeper. Until the backs of her legs hit the bed, and the impact jolted her mouth from his. He stared at her a moment before he slowly kneeled, pulling her undies and pants off her ankles as he nipped and licked her knees, making her jerk and laugh.

"Stop that," she said. "My knees are ticklish."

He grasped her calves as his tongue slipped across the inside of one knee, then the other, interspersed with tiny nibbles. "How ticklish?"

"Very." She gasped and wriggled, the sensation of his teeth and tongue on her bones and skin both sensitive and exciting. "And if you don't stop, it's not my fault if my reflexes send one up to crack you in the jaw."

"Risk noted." His hands slipped up to widen her legs as his tongue moved on in a shivery path to her inner thighs. "But I think we already agreed that life is full of risk. If it's potentially dangerous to taste you all over, then, believe me, that's a risk I'm more than happy to take."

Her breath coming in embarrassing little pants now as he moved northward, she knew it was time to change direction. While part of her wanted, more than anything, for his mouth to keep going to the part of her currently quivering in anticipation, it seemed that mutual pleasure was more in order.

"Come up here and kiss me." She placed her hands on his smooth shoulders, trying to tug him back up.

"I am kissing you." And, boy, he sure was. His lips were pressing inch by torturous inch against her shivering flesh.

"My mouth. Kiss my mouth." She tugged harder at his shoulders. If she didn't get him away from where he was headed, she knew she just might combust. "I'm the one who's supposed to be administering TLC here, remember?"

He lifted his gaze to hers. His eyes were heavy-lidded with desire, but touched with amusement, too, and the smile he gave her was full of pure, masculine satisfaction. "For some reason, I forgot. Probably because I'm already feeling much less stressed. But if it will make you happy, who am I to argue?"

With one last kiss so high on her inner thigh she nearly groaned, he got to his feet. Which reminded her he still had his pants on, while she was sitting there utterly naked. His gaze traveled across every inch of her skin, hot enough to scorch, and she was a little surprised that his perusal was exciting instead of embarrassing.

She reached for his pants and undid them, happy that he took charge and quickly finished off the job. Then stared at the now very visible confirmation that he was every bit as aroused as she was.

"So now what, Dr. Girard?" He placed his hands on the bed, flanking her hips, and leaned close. "The TLC ball is in your court."

She gulped. All the things she'd fantasized about seemed to have vacated her mind, along with every rational thought. Except how much she wanted to grab him and pull him on top of her and feel him deep inside.

"I...I can't remember exactly what I had in mind to soothe you and make you feel better. Give me a minute."

"That's okay," he said between pressing soft kisses to her mouth. "As I said, I already feel a whole lot better. Expecting to feel even better real soon."

His strong hands wrapped around her waist and he lifted her up to him, nudging her legs around his waist as he kissed her again. She was vaguely aware of the sound of the covers being yanked back and the cool sheets touching her skin at the same time Jack's hot body covered hers.

"I've realized the one thing that will soothe me the most," he whispered against her lips.

"What?"

"Making you feel good." He kissed her again. His body was deliciously heavy on hers as his hands stroked her everywhere, exciting and tantalizing. Their kiss grew deeper, wilder as his talented fingers finally delved into her moist core until she feared he might bring her to climax with just his touch.

Then the sudden, harsh ring of her hotel phone startled them both, sending their teeth clacking together. "Holy hell!" Jack frowned. "Are you okay?"

With her breath still short, she slid her fingers across his moist lips. "No blood, I don't think. You?"

"Fine. More than fine." His eyes gleamed into hers. "Except for the damned interruption just when things were getting very...soothing."

She chuckled breathily as they both turned their heads to the still-ringing phone.

"Do you need to get that?" he asked.

Was he kidding? Even if it was the French president, she wasn't about to talk on the phone at that moment.

"Whoever it is will leave a message. Or call back. Now, where were we?" She reached for him, squeezed, and the moan he gave in response sent her heart pumping faster and her legs around his waist in silent invitation.

He quickly ripped open a condom. "About to get to the next step in making us both feel good," he said, grasping her hips as they joined. Slowly, wonderfully, but as the tension grew she had to urge him to move faster, deeper. The room seemed to spin dizzily like the carousel had, but this time there were no barriers between them. She held on tight, loving the taste of him and the feel of him, until she cried out in release, wrenching a deep groan from his chest as he followed.

Jack buried his face in her neck, their gasping breaths seeming loud in the quiet of the room. Until another sound disturbed her bone-melting, utter relaxation and tranquility—the muffled ringing of a cell phone.

Jack lifted his head and looked down at the floor with a frown. "Who the hell keeps bothering us? I hope nothing's happened at the hospital."

He dropped a kiss on her mouth, lingering there, before he got up and dug his phone from the pocket of his discarded pants. Avery enjoyed the very sexy view of him, standing there comfortably naked, his skin covered with a sheen of sweat.

"Dr. Dunbar."

She watched his frown deepen and sat up, beginning to get alarmed. Hopefully this wasn't a crisis with a patient.

"And you can't give me some idea what this is about now?" he asked. "Fine. I'll be there."

"What is it?"

"I don't know." His warm body lay next to hers

again, propped on his elbow. "Bob Timkin wants to meet with me—with both of us—tomorrow morning at eight. Says he has to talk to me right away about something to do with the trial."

"What? Why?"

"He wouldn't say. You don't happen to know, do you?"

The pleasure of the evening began to fade at the expression on his face. Beyond serious. Maybe even a touch suspicious? She couldn't even imagine how he'd react if he knew Crilex had given her the power to shut down the trial if she deemed it necessary, and the thought chilled her formerly very toasty body. "No. I don't. If I did, I'd tell you."

"Did you tell him you were concerned about the number of patients who've had the valve leak? You know I feel strongly that we haven't treated nearly enough patients to make any kind of judgment on that yet."

"Of course I didn't speak with him about Mr. Arnoult. For one thing, I haven't had a chance to finish compiling the data on his...situation. And I also told you I know the valve design was not why he died."

A long sigh left him before his mouth touched hers with a sweet, tender connection at odds with the tense tone of his voice. His finger tracked down her cheek before he slipped from the bed and got dressed, his expression impassive when he turned to her.

"I wish mixing...this...with work didn't create a hell of a complication for both of us. But there's no getting around it that it does." He stepped to the bed and took her chin in his hand, tilting her face up for another soft kiss. "Thank you for the TLC tonight. Sweet dreams."

And then he was gone, the door closing behind him

with a sharp click. A whirl of emotions filled her chest, and she didn't know which one took center stage in her heart. Frustration that he still clearly didn't completely trust her to report the data scientifically and not emotionally? Disappointment, even sadness, that this obvious "thing" they had between them was a huge problem because of their jobs? Anxiety, knowing he would definitely not like having been kept in the dark about her authority to decide if the trial was rolled out further or not?

She flopped back onto the bed, her body still feeling the remnants of their lovemaking, and remembered how wonderful every second of it had felt.

Now, instead of stealing a kiss or two with him tomorrow, she knew the smart thing to do was go back to a strictly professional friendship. And she also had to wonder what in the world Bob Timkin had planned.

CHAPTER TEN

JACK SWALLOWED THE last of his morning coffee, wishing it didn't make him think of Avery and how her mouth always tasted after they'd shared espresso. Made him think of that first morning they'd spent together, that entire, magical day, and how beautiful and adorable she'd been. Realizing, from that moment on, he'd been fascinated by her in every way. Her looks, her brains, her personality.

He couldn't shake that fascination and attraction. An attraction that had grown even deeper after their time together last night, making love again to her beautiful body. Except his heart rate had barely slowed when the phone call had come, bringing a lot of questions with it. A harsh reminder of what he kept forgetting whenever he was with her. Which was that mixing business with pleasure was always one hell of a bad idea, no matter how incredible that pleasure was.

He thought he'd learned that painful lesson all too well. A lesson that had come in the form of doubt cast on his professional character and integrity, resulting in some very personal questions from a hospital ethics board. A lesson in why he should never get involved with a woman connected in any way with his work.

Except he knew Avery was nothing like Vanessa. She wasn't the kind of woman who would advance her own career at the expense of someone else's.

He took the elevator to the hospital's administrative offices on the top floor, where Bob had a nice, cushy office that someone had clearly given up for him. About to knock on the doorjamb, he was surprised to hear Avery's voice speaking through the partially open door, then the rumble of Bob's voice in answer.

He knocked on the door and didn't wait to be asked in before pushing it all the way open to step inside. Timkin looked up, then stood, a broad smile on his face. "Jack. Thanks for coming. Have a seat."

"I'm good standing, thanks."

"Dr. Girard was just updating me on the patient data from the trial so far."

"Seems impossible to have any kind of real report, considering we've operated on all of twelve patients so far."

"Well, yes. But all of them came through it nicely, I see."

"Actually, that's not entirely true," Avery said. "Several of the patients have had significant paravalvular regurgitation, as Dr. Dunbar and I have discussed."

"And in that discussion I noted that a certain percentage of patients are expected to have that complication and can live fine with it." His chest began to burn a little. Was she about to tell Timkin she thought there might be a flaw in the design? He was confident that Bob was completely behind this trial and the next phase of the rollout to other hospitals.

"We do know that is a normal, and expected, complication, Dr. Girard," Timkin said. "While I'm aware the numbers of patients experiencing that are currently slightly higher than we would have wished, the procedure hasn't been done on nearly enough patients for those numbers to be meaningful."

Jack relaxed a little, and he waited to hear why Timkin had called the meeting. Avery's brows were lowered in a frown, and he could practically see the wheels spinning in that brain of hers, probably coming up with various data she wanted to spout.

"Which is why I asked you both to come here this morning," Timkin said. "We've decided to significantly increase the number of patients in this clinical trial, which I'm sure will please you, Jack."

"What do you mean, you want to increase the number of patients in the trial?" Avery asked, her eyes wide.

"It seems logical to me that we get as many patients in the trial as we can for these last two and a half weeks," Timkin said. "We need as much data as possible before we decide how many hospitals to roll this out to next. I have a few of my people looking for good patient candidates and screening them as we speak, and of course I'd like your nurse to work on finding some, as well."

"Frankly, I don't think that's a good idea," Avery said. Her gaze flicked to Jack, then away, before she continued. "With the comparatively high percentage of the prosthetic valves experiencing leakage, I think the trial should be conducted on a smaller number of patients so we can keep our eye on that until we know more."

"I respect your opinion, Dr. Girard. But increasing the numbers can't be anything but good, giving us the conclusive data we all want."

Jack smiled at this great news. "I appreciate the vote of confidence, Bob. Dr. Girard is, of course, the leading expert on this device but isn't as familiar with patient care. Those in the trial experiencing the valve leakage are all doing well as we manage their situation."

As he turned to leave, his gaze paused on Avery, and he was surprised to see the look on her face was completely different from that of a moment ago. Instead of concern, her green eyes held deep disappointment. He'd even call it hurt. Was it because of what he'd said when he'd reassured Bob he had the leakages under control?

This trial was beyond important to him, the patients it was helping and the future of interventional cardiology. Avery knew that as well as anybody. Why she was so overly concerned about the valve leakage, he didn't understand and refused to worry about yet.

But as he headed to the cath lab, the image of the hurt in her eyes went along with him.

Jack headed for the hotel fitness room, needing a physical release from another long day at the hospital, his muscles tense from hours of standing on his feet doing surgeries. He had to give Crilex credit—they'd gotten additional patients lined up incredibly fast, and he and Jessica had been working flat out. Which he welcomed for the clinical trial and welcomed for himself.

The busy pace had left him with little time to think about Avery. During the brief moments he'd had free, though, she'd been on his mind. Thinking about all the great things he'd learned about her over the past weeks. Knowing she wasn't the kind of self-interested person who would skew data to benefit her career, and feeling bad that had even crossed his mind. They might not always agree, but the woman had absolute integrity.

That it seemed he'd accidentally hurt her made him feel like crap. Made him want to head to her room and apologize, then grab her to explore more of Paris and laugh together. Kiss and make love together. That desire was so strong he could only hope that running hard on the treadmill would somehow blank it all from his mind.

At 9:00 p.m. there were only two other people in the exercise room, and he was glad he wouldn't have to wait around for any of the machines or weights to become available. He slung a towel around his neck and started out jogging on the treadmill, increasing the pace until he was running, breathing hard, sweating. To his disgust, even that didn't stop his thoughts from drifting to Avery. To the softness of her skin and the taste of it on his tongue. To her laugh and the amazing green of her eyes.

Which made him one damned confused man. He adjusted the treadmill settings and picked up the pace, noticing out of the corner of his eye that the middle-aged man who had been lifting crazily heavy weights was now sitting strangely sideways on the bench, leaning on one hand.

Jack looked more carefully at him, realizing the guy didn't look like he felt very well. He slowed to a stop, quickly wiped the sweat from his face and walked over to the man, concerned at the ashen color of his face.

"You okay?"

The man shook his head and laboriously said a few words in French. Jack hoped like hell he could at least understand a little English, even if he couldn't speak it. "I'm a doctor. I'm going to check your pulse."

Thankfully, he nodded, and Jack pressed his fingers to the man's wrist to see if his heart was in a normal sinus rhythm. It was fast, very fast, and he'd begun to sweat buckets, too, neither of which were signs of anything good. Just as Jack was about to ask the man if he thought he might be having a heart attack he slumped sideways and started sliding clear off the bench.

"Whoa!" Jack was able to grab him midway, managing to keep him from cracking his head on the hard floor.

"What is wrong, monsieur?" The other person in the room had come to stand next to him, staring.

"Get the hotel to call the medical squad."

The guy ran off just as the man opened his eyes again, thank the Lord. His brows lowered as he blinked at Jack, saying something Jack wished he could understand. Pressing his fingers to the man's wrist again, he grimly noted his pulse was thready, which meant his blood pressure was high, which again meant nothing good.

"Good God, Jack, what's wrong?" To his surprise, Avery crouched next to him, deep concern on her face as she looked from the ill man to him.

"I think he's having the big one. Going in and out of V-fib, and his pulse is really tachy." He looked up at her, relieved she might be able to communicate with the man. "Ask him how he's feeling, where it hurts."

She quickly spoke to the man in French and he managed to answer her back. "He says he's nauseated and his chest feels strange."

"Damn. The chances of this not being a heart attack are slim to none." He scanned the room and didn't see what he'd hoped for. "I wish this place had a defibrillator. His arrhythmia is bad, and if he crashes, I don't think CPR's going to do it."

"They do. Over here." She ran around the other side of the L-shaped room and returned with exactly what he needed if the man went into true V-fib.

"How did you know that was there? I've been in this gym ten times and never noticed."

"It's by the plié bar, which I'm guessing you don't use."

She gave him a quick grin, and he grinned back before turning to place his fingers against the man's carotid artery. "You'd guess right. I—"

With a sudden, strangled sound the man, who'd been lying on his side, flopped onto his back, obviously unconscious again. Jack shook him, then rubbed his knuckles against the man's sternum. "Hey, buddy! Wake up. Can you hear me? Wake up!"

But the guy just lay there like he was dead, and Jack cursed. "We've got to get his shirt off so I can check his heart rate with the defib."

They wrestled the T-shirt off the man as quickly as they could, then Jack grabbed the defibrillator. Both moved fast to get the paddle wires untwined as he pressed them to the man's chest. Then stared at the EKG monitor on the paddle in disbelief.

"He's code blue. I'm going to have to bust him." He looked up at her tense face. "Can you set it at three hundred joules while I get it placed? Then get the hell out of the way."

She nodded and her fingers got it adjusted impressively fast.

"Okay. Ready? Clear!"

She jumped up and backpedaled as Jack sent the electricity to the man's heart.

Nothing.

"Clear again." His own heart pounding like he'd just jumped off the treadmill, he busted the man once more. When the man's chest heaved and his eyelids flickered, then opened, Jack exhaled a deep breath he hadn't even realized he'd been holding in his lungs.

"Thank God," he heard Avery say devoutly as she came back and kneeled next to them, reaching to hold the man's hand.

"Yeah." Jack pressed his fingers to the man's throat. "Pulse is down to ninety. And his color's even a little better. I think we did it, Dr. Girard."

Their eyes met briefly across the poor, supine guy, and a wordless communication went between them. Relief that they'd been able to help and joy that he was hopefully out of the woods.

The man weakly said something in French, and Avery smiled and answered before turning to Jack. "He asked what happened. I told him his heart stopped, and you saved his life."

"We saved his life. You were awesome."

Her smile widened before she turned back to speak to the man again, and Jack could see her squeezing his hand. Now that he could take a minute to breathe, he had to marvel at how calm she'd been through the whole thing, and how comforting him obviously came as second nature to her. Doctors and nurses were trained how to react to this kind of crisis, but he doubted there was a lot of that kind of education in biomedical PhD school.

The door to the fitness room clattered open as several emergency medical techs wheeled in a gurney. The guy who'd run from the room to get help followed, along with several people Jack recognized as hotel management. He stood and updated the med techs on what had happened and where the man's heart rate was now.

The hotel guys talked with Avery. She handed them the defibrillator, and he heard her saying what a hero Jack was. Part of him absolutely hated that, since he was no hero. He was a doctor who'd been in the right place when he'd been needed.

But another part of him couldn't be unhappy about Avery praising him that way. The hotel staff pumped his hand and thanked him, and he repeated that it was just lucky he'd been in the right place and gave them credit for having the defibrillator there for him to use. If they hadn't, he was certain the outcome would not have been good for the man.

It seemed the room went from full of people to empty in a matter of minutes, and he noticed what he'd missed before in all the excitement. Avery wearing tiny, sexy exercise shorts that showed off her toned legs and a tank top that revealed a whole lot more of her skin than he'd ever been able to see before, since she was always dressed for the cold or the hospital.

Well, except for their two blissful moments together, when he'd been privileged to see every inch of her body.

His heart went into a little atrial fibrillation of its own at the memories and the current vision standing right in front of him.

"That was one lucky man," Avery said. "How many people have a cardiologist around when they're having a heart attack? Were you in here working out when it happened?"

"I was running on the treadmill. Trying to loosen my

muscles." *Trying to forget about you.* "He was lucky all right. Lucky that you came in when you did and that you knew where the machine was. I've got to tell you, I'm pretty impressed at how calm and cool you were, helping with what needed to happen without freaking out."

"Believe me, I was freaking out on the inside." She grinned. "But that's a sweet thing for you to say. Much better than the stinging barbs you've thrown lately."

"Listen." He rubbed his hand across the back of his neck to loosen the knots there. Hoped she'd accept his apology. "I'm sorry I said you didn't know much about patient care. I'm sure you do. I just wanted Bob to know the leakages so far are minor, but I shouldn't have implied you're clueless about postoperative treatment."

"No, you shouldn't have. I may not be a medical doctor or nurse, but gathering the data teaches me plenty, believe me."

"I'm sure it does." He cupped her chin in his hand because he wanted that connection. Wanted to show her he truly cared how she felt. "Did it hurt you when I said that?"

"Honestly? To my core." Her words pricked his heart, but the sweet smile she gave him soothed the wound. "Though I just might have not very nicely accused you of certain things, as well. Like maybe you were sleeping with a married woman the same week you were kissing me."

"You know, you're right. That wasn't nice of you at all." He caught her elbows in his hands, tugging her against him. "So we're even."

"Even."

As he looked into the green of her eyes he tried hard to conjure all the reasons he had to keep a professional distance from her. But he couldn't. All he could think about was how much he enjoyed kissing her and making love with her, and how he wanted more of all of it.

"What is it about you that makes it impossible for me to keep a professional distance? Even when I try?" he asked, genuinely baffled.

"Maybe because we share a love of espresso?"

"Maybe," he said, dipping his head down to speak against her lips. "Or maybe it's just you."

"No." She shook her head, her lips slipping back and forth across his mouth as she did, and that simple touch nearly made him groan. "It's us. That mysterious and unexplainable chemistry, whether we like it or not."

"Sometimes not," he said. "But I find I can't help that, way more often, I like it very much."

Knowing he damned well shouldn't, he kissed her, loving the way she instantly melted against him, her arms sliding around his back to hold him tight. Their mouths and tongues moved in a slow dance that already felt seductively familiar. A tiny little sound came from her throat as the kiss deepened, a sound so full of desire it sent his blood pumping and nearly had him slipping his hands into those tiny shorts she was wearing, not caring at all about the consequences.

Somehow, though, he managed to summon every ounce of inner strength he had to break the kiss, dragging in a few desperate breaths to clear his head. Not only were they in a public place, which seemed to always be a problem whenever he kissed her, but nothing had really changed.

The chemistry—hell, more like a nuclear reaction—was most definitely there. But so was the inescapable conflict in their jobs. And that situation was one harsh reality.

"Right now, there's nothing I'd like more in the world than for us to head upstairs and take up where we left off a few nights ago," he said, and the truth of that statement nearly had him grabbing her hand, hightailing it to his room and acting on exactly what he wanted. "But that would just make our jobs more difficult. The work I'm doing here is damned important to me. And I know your work is important to you."

"It is. Which is why I'm going to stretch on the bar, then get running. Good night, Jack." She rose on her toes to give him a quick peck on the cheek and turned to walk to the plié bar.

The sight of her sexy rear in those shorts and the thought of how she might contort herself around that bar practically made him groan. A mini war raged in his chest, with the part of him that wanted her yesterday, today and tomorrow fighting with the cool, rational part of his brain that seemed to short-circuit every time he was around her.

He thought about pretending to continue his workout while really watching whatever she was about to do, but he managed to move to the elevator instead. Giving work one hundred percent of his focus was something he'd been good at for a long time. Time to get with that program and somehow forget the vision of Avery's shapely butt cheeks peeking from beneath those shorts.

Yeah. Like that was going to happen. Which made him wonder. How cold, exactly, could he get the shower in his room?

CHAPTER ELEVEN

JACK STARED IN frustration at the Doppler echocardiogram. The paravalvular regurgitation from the prosthetic valve was more than obvious. The valve looked
like it was fitting tightly, but there was no denying the
image of the fluid seeping slightly from around it. Why
had the past two patients experienced this problem when
it hadn't been an issue with the last ten?

"What do you think, Jack?" Jessica asked, peering
over his shoulder at the echocardiogram.

"I don't know what to think. I'm trying to figure out
if I somehow did something different with these two
patients. Maybe I'm not being careful enough as I insert the cath to remove the diseased valve. Or when I
place the new one."

Jessica shook her head. "I'm watching almost every
second you're working, and if I'd noticed you doing
anything different at all, I'd say so."

His mind spun back to past procedures, wondering
if the increased patient load had made him hurry in
any way. He didn't think so, but he would be extra
careful from now on to be sure to take his time and tri-
ple-check the monitor as he was putting the prosthetic
valve in place.

\

Jessica glanced around, then leaned close, speaking in a near whisper. "Do you think it's a design flaw, like Dr. Girard has been worried about all along?"

His chest tightened. He'd have to be as stubborn as a mule to not have wondered exactly that. "I don't know. It's possible. The percentage of patients with medically manageable leakage is more than we expected, but not dramatically more. We're just going to have to wait and see the numbers as the trial unfolds."

Jessica nodded. "This patient's pulmonary edema is improving nicely, and the liquid from her Foley is crystal-clear now. She's going to be fine, I think."

"Good. I'll check on her again this afternoon."

"Dr. Dunbar!"

He and Jessica both turned to the nurse who'd run in. "Yes?"

"Madame Belisle is having trouble breathing. I fear it may be another aortic insufficiency."

He stiffened. Another one? Damn it to hell. "We'll be right there."

Jack grimly strode to Mrs. Belisle's room, with Jessica right behind. When he saw that Avery was in there, standing by the patient's bed, his heart knocked hard in his chest. He wasn't sure if it was from seeing her, or if it was because he knew she was taking notes on the third patient with this problem in a matter of days.

He took the woman's pulse, checked her blood pressure and went through the process to confirm the diagnosis, but it was pretty clear. Same song, different verse, and he hated that they had no idea why this kept happening at this rate.

As he gave orders to Jessica and the other nurse, he was painfully aware of Avery observing all of it, tapping away at her tablet. Watching as the patient received the medications needed to reduce her blood pressure, the diuretic to clear her lungs and the Foley catheter to catch the fluids. Continued tapping away as the portable echocardiogram was brought to the room to get images of Mrs. Belisle's heart activity.

He resolutely ignored her presence, concentrating on the situation. A half hour later, relieved that the patient was breathing a little easier, Jack let himself glance up at Avery, surprised to see her green eyes staring straight into his. This time there wasn't a hint of the humor he loved to see there. They were beyond serious.

"I'm going to look at the echocardiogram," he said to no one in particular. He knew his voice was gruff, but he couldn't help the slightly sick feeling in his gut that maybe this clinical trial was heading downhill fast.

"I'd like to look at it with you, Dr. Dunbar," Avery's voice said from behind him as he moved down the hall.

Of course she would.

His gut tightened a little more. No matter how disturbing all this was, though, he knew he couldn't blame her or feel ticked at her. She was doing her job and, ultimately, if it turned out she'd been right all along, he had to accept that. Should welcome it, really, because if the device was truly flawed, he wouldn't want to put patients at risk any more than she did. If he had to spend another year working with Crilex's biomedical engineers to improve it before testing it on humans again, then that's what would have to happen.

Way premature to be thinking like that, Jack fiercely reminded himself. This clinical trial was only half over, and it was very possible they'd just had a run of bad luck and the next twenty patients would all do fine.

"What are you thinking, Jack?" Avery asked quietly as they studied the Doppler echocardiogram of Mrs. Belisle and the obvious, slight leakage from around the valve.

He looked at her, measuring his response. He trusted her. He did. But loose lips sank ships, as the old saying went, and there was too much riding on this trial to jeopardize it by being too forthcoming with the woman who'd been concerned about this risk all along.

"I'm thinking that I will carefully examine how I'm inserting the catheter and device. As I do that, we'll continue to compile the data. We're also going to perform the procedure on all the very sick patients who've lined up to receive it. Even those with this complication will be better off than they were before the surgery, you know."

"So you're not worried that this is clear evidence the device design just isn't yet where it needs to be?"

The expression on her face showed loud and clear that's what she thought, with maybe a little contempt thrown in. Or was it disappointment? Either way, he didn't want to see it and turned his attention back to the monitor. "Too soon to say. There's not enough evidence, and worrying about it when we don't have the data from a full study is pointless."

She was silent for so long, with such an odd, thoughtful expression as she studied him, it made him jittery. When he couldn't stand it any longer, he abruptly turned. "I have some other patients to see."

"Jack."

He paused and looked back at her, bracing himself for a lecture, willing himself to not let his frustration over all this send his temper flaring. "Yes?"

"I have a great idea," she said, her voice suddenly, surprisingly, light and playful. The same voice she'd used that first, very memorable day they'd spent together.

"Sounds scary."

"Not scary. I think you'll like the proposal I have in mind."

That mischievous smile that usually made him smile back was in her eyes once more. Right now, though, it made him wonder why her demeanor had changed so abruptly. He folded his arms and waited.

"You've been working long and hard and don't have any patients scheduled this weekend. You're looking pretty haggard, which is going to worry your little old lady patients who think you're the most handsome thing in the world."

"You think?" He actually did smile at that, and how she managed to change the entire atmosphere of the room in one minute, he didn't know. "Is that what's called a backhanded compliment?"

"Maybe. So here's my proposal." She moved closer to him and pressed her hands to his chest. He felt some of his stress seep away at their warmth through his scrubs, at how good they felt there.

It made him realize how much he'd missed her touch. Missed touching her.

He let himself cup her waist with his hands because he wanted to, and she was the one who'd started the touching after all. "Does it have anything to do with espresso? If it does, a triple sounds pretty good right now."

"It might." Her smile could only be described as flirtatious, which ratcheted up Jack's interest tenfold. At the same time, he felt even more perplexed. "I promise some serious espresso consumption if you agree. Wine consumption, too."

"Wine consumption? You sure know how to intrigue a guy. What other guilty pleasures might be included in this proposal?"

"You'll find out, if you just say, 'Yes, Avery.'" Her coy words were accompanied by the sparkle in her eyes he'd fallen for the first day they'd met, oddly mingling with a tinge of seriousness.

"I never say yes until I know what I'm agreeing to. What's the catch, and is it going to hurt much?"

"It might hurt, but you're tough enough to handle it," she said, the sparkle fading a bit. "I'd like you to come to Alsace with me, to a little village northeast of Paris. Not too far and easy to get to by train. It's beyond beautiful, so I'll get to show you more of France, and you'll get to shake the dust of this place from your feet and be all refreshed when you come back to work."

He tipped his head to study her, trying to figure out where she was going with this. "Despite the wine consumption promise, I suspect you're not inviting me there for a weekend of sightseeing and wild sex." Though just thinking about spending two days alone with her sent a hot zing through every nerve ending, which he quickly tamped down. Hadn't he sworn off sex or anything else with her?

Yeah, right. If that was her proposal, he'd be saying yes in half of one second and to hell with the consequences.

"Maybe it is about wild sex," she said, giving him the adorable teasing look he'd missed almost as much as her touch, and his heart pumped harder. "Along with meeting the patient I mentioned before, who was one of the first to receive my original TAVI device. I'd like you to hear his story."

"Uh-huh." Here was the damned big letdown he'd known was coming. "How about we go for the wild sex and forget the rest?"

"It's a package deal. We'll be out of Paris and away from the hospital to relax."

"You want me to meet this guy so much you'll risk more of us mixing business with pleasure?" The part of him that wanted his hands and mouth on her again was already yelling yes, but going there with her would be one bad idea. "I know the problems patients with leaky valves live with, Avery. And much as I'd like nothing better than to go on a weekend away with you, it'd just complicate an already complicated situation."

To his shock, she reached up to wrap her arms around his neck and kissed him. Kissed him until his knees nearly buckled and his heart raced. Kissed him until he couldn't breathe and his stress had completely evaporated. Kissed him until he'd say yes to pretty much anything she asked.

When she finally stopped, he could see in her eyes the same delirious desire he felt pumping through every cell in his body. Even though she was obviously using her all-too-irresistible feminine wiles to get him to see that guy, it was also clear she was every bit as turned on as he was.

"How about it, Jack?" she whispered against his lips. "I know you need a break. And meeting this man will just add to your data, so there's nothing to lose. Except, maybe, your virtue."

"Pretty sure I lost my virtue that first day we met."

He had to chuckle, but he shook his head, not quite believing her tactics. "You drive a very hard bargain, Dr. Girard."

She pressed closer against him, and when his erection pressed into her stomach she gave him the wickedest smile. "Very hard, Dr. Dunbar. Which I hope means your answer is yes."

In a sign that this trip just might go as well as Avery hoped, the gray clouds parted and the sun cast its golden fingers across the vineyards and snowy mountains that surrounded Riquewihr. Jack parked the little rental car outside the town's ancient walls and turned to her with a smile.

"This place is amazing," he said. "I can't believe that one minute we're driving through endless vineyards, then all of a sudden here's this beautiful old medieval town parked right in the middle of it all."

"You should see it in the summertime, when everything's green and flowers are everywhere," she said, glad he already seemed to like this place. "Wait till we get inside the walls. The town itself is every bit as amazing and lovely."

She smiled, pleased that he again looked like the upbeat man she'd met in the hotel that very first day, and not the cardiologist whose tense and tired expression the past week had made her want to gather him up and hold him and give him more of that TLC she'd promised him before. It wasn't good for his patients or for Jack if he worked endless hours under stress, and in a sudden decision not too different from the moment she'd first met him in the hotel, she'd wanted to do something about it.

For days, a disturbing feeling had nagged at her. As the number of patients in the trial had more than doubled, the problems had increased, too. She knew Jack was as concerned about it as she was. But she also knew him well enough to guess that his fatigue and worry would turn into defensiveness if she suggested again that he ratchet the trial back to its original numbers, or even fewer.

Inspiration had struck on how she could accomplish two things at once. Get him to come here to Riquewihr for a much-needed break—and to meet Benjamin Larue. A lovely man with a lovely family, whose life had been damaged irreversibly during the first TAVI trials.

Jack's loose stride already seemed much more relaxed than the fast pace he kept in the hospital, moving from surgeries to patients to various test results and back. They headed toward the old clock tower, walking through the gate beneath it in the ancient wall.

"How many times have you been here?" he asked. "Just in the summertime?"

"I've been here twice. Once in winter and once in summer. Totally different things to do, of course. I love to hike the mountains, but the snow cover at the moment requires a different approach. So I figured maybe we'd cross-country ski or snowshoe. Have you ever tried it? I made a reservation for us just a half hour from now, so we'll have to hurry to get there. Unless you'd rather do something else."

"I haven't tried either one." He leaned closer, the devilish smile that had knocked her socks off—among other things—back in full force and electrifying the air. "But I'm all for any kind of exercise you might think up to get our blood pumping."

Her blood was already pumping just from looking at him and thinking about the kind of physical exercise he obviously had on his mind.

The curve of his lips, the light in his eyes as he looked at her and the various landmarks they passed reminded her so much of the Jack she'd shown around Paris that first day. The Jack she'd tumbled into bed with, before she'd thought long enough about it. Before she'd found out exactly how ill-advised that decision had turned out to be.

But pretending that hadn't happened, and deciding not to let it happen again, had come to seem pretty pointless. When the trial was over and she'd studied the data, her recommendation to Crilex would be the same no matter whether they were sleeping together or not. She knew Jack wanted what was best for the patients, and she had to believe, either way it went, that he'd come to the same conclusion she did.

She smirked at herself. Like before, she seemed to have a much easier time talking herself into being with him than the other way around. Probably because he looked sexier in scrubs than about anybody she'd ever seen, and asking her to not think about stripping them off him to see that lean, muscular body of his was like asking her to give up coffee.

She glanced at him out of the corner of her eye, smiling at the memory of his shocked expression as she'd coerced him to come on this trip. She'd never tried seducing someone to get them on board with a different agenda. Now she knew it was pretty exciting to know how well her sex appeal apparently worked on the man.

They walked down a cobbled street flanked by beautiful medieval buildings, with Jack commenting on all of it in amazement, before they checked into their small hotel. From the moment she'd first seen the place she'd been awed and delighted by the beautiful pastel blues, yellows and mauves of the buildings, like something from a fairy tale.

"Some cities in France had to rebuild after World War II, so a lot of the buildings are really replicas rather than the original medieval structures," she said. "I'm told that only two bombs dropped here, though, so it's nearly all original. Isn't the whole place incredible?"

"It is. I've never seen anything like it."

Pleasure fluttered inside her at the fact that he liked it as much as she did. As they made their way down the narrow, stone-lined hallway, Jack smiled at her. "Gotta tell you, the whole town reminds me of a Hollywood movie set."

"I know what you mean." The first time she had come here, she had thought the Renaissance-style stone and half-timber homes were almost too enchanting to believe. "I've always wondered if the animators who did *Beauty and the Beast* came here for inspiration."

"I confess I haven't watched that movie and also confess I hope that's not part of your agenda for the weekend." He shoved open their room door and looked down at her with the teasing humor she'd enjoyed that first day they met. Humor that had been in short supply the past week. "Or watching *The Sound of Music*. Have to wonder if that's the plan, though, considering the dirndl that you're wearing."

"Dirndl?" She set her suitcase on the floor and fisted her hands on her hips, giving him a mock glare. "My dress is not a dirndl, Dr. Dunbar. It's a blouse beneath a corduroy jumper."

"If you say so." He reached to unbutton her coat, pulling it apart to look at her dress. "No need to get defensive, though. I like it. A lot."

He ran his finger along the lacy top of her blouse that dipped low to just above her breasts. Avery looked down, watching the track of his finger, her breath growing short. Vaguely, she pondered that maybe the skirt did look a little like a dirndl. Her main thoughts, though, were that his touch felt wonderful, that she'd missed it, and that, unlike the first two times they'd briefly shared a hotel room, she didn't feel at all nervous. All she felt was a delicious anticipation of the day and night they'd be spending together.

She looked back up at him, and a warm flush crept through her body at the way he was looking at her. The small smile was still on his face, but his eyes were filled with something entirely different that told her he, too, was feeling that same breathless anticipation.

"Bonjour, monsieur...mademoiselle."

They both turned to the open door and saw an older gentleman with a wide, curled mustache smiling at them. "I wanted to suggest that you join us this evening at five o'clock for a wine tasting from our local vineyards. There will be complimentary hors d'oeuvres as well, in our wine cellar."

"Thank you," Jack said. "We haven't made any plans yet, but that sounds great."

He shoved the door closed behind the man and turned to her again. "Are you sure Riquewihr isn't just some elaborate Hollywood hoax? I mean, how often do you see a guy with a mustache like that outside the movies?"

Her laugh morphed into more of a little hiccup when his fingers tugged apart the lapels of her coat again.

"So," he asked in a low voice, "are we staying in or going out?"

"I…um…" She struggled to decide, wanting to show him the amazing and wonderful things about Riquewihr during the daylight hours of this single Saturday that they had. Wanted to enjoy the same delight she'd felt, that she was sure they'd both felt, seeing the Eiffel Tower and the Sacré Coeur. Have those kinds of lovely moments before they stopped at the Larue family winery to meet Benjamin.

But she also wanted that heady give and take they'd had before. The overwhelming sensations when they let go of all the external problems, shared their bodies and simply let the chemistry between them ignite into a searing, physical passion like none other she'd ever experienced.

She drew a breath to try to finish her sentence, but it was a shaky one at best. Because it was clear he could read exactly what she'd been thinking, and she nearly caught fire just from the look in his eyes before he lowered his head.

His lips covered hers, teasing, tasting, as his hands moved to her waist. Slid up to cup her breasts, his fingers again brushing the filmy top of her blouse as he deepened the kiss, the sweep of his tongue so delicious she had to bite back a moan.

When he broke the kiss, his eyes were so heavy-lidded she could barely see the gleam in the darkness of his eyes. "Didn't you say we have a time schedule to hit the mountain for a little skiing or snowshoeing?"

She nodded, knowing any verbal answer she gave at that moment would just come out as a whisper until she caught her breath. "Yes," she finally managed. "I thought you'd enjoy the fresh air and how gorgeous it is up there. But we don't have to. We have the day off to do whatever makes us happy."

"Just being with you makes me happy," he said, and she was surprised the words didn't hold a sensual tone. They sounded beyond sincere, and her heart tripped in her chest. "And since we have only so many hours of daylight, I think we should do what you'd already planned for us. Because I sure haven't been disappointed in any of our activities in France so far, Ms. Tour Guide."

She stared at Jack and realized he was being utterly genuine. He truly enjoyed just being with her, here or in Paris or wherever they happened to be, and hadn't come here with her just for the "wild sex" she'd teased him with. As she thought back to her two previous relationships, she realized that the physical part of them had been the primary element.

Which wasn't at all what she had with Jack. What they had between them went deeper than the sexual chemistry they'd talked about, which was thrilling and scary at the same time. Because she knew his job was not just his priority, it was his life. She was a brief interlude in that life—an interlude he'd made clear he felt uncomfortable participating in.

And if it became necessary to halt the trial, she could only hope and pray he understood why.

Her heart giving an odd little twist, she gave him a soft kiss before grasping his hand and smiling into his beautiful eyes. "Then let's head to the Vosges mountains. I think you'll love it, and afterward we'll both be more than ready for a little après-ski."

"Lead on, Dr. Girard. I'm all yours."

CHAPTER TWELVE

"EVEN WITHOUT THE potential for wine and wild sex,
I'm glad I agreed to this trip," Jack said, looking handsome as all get-out with his cheeks flushed and his dark
hair poking from beneath his knit hat. "Growing up, a
few of my friends went skiing in the winter with their
families. Both downhill and cross-country. We never
went places like that, but now I wish I'd tried this kind
of thing at home."

"I knew you'd like it." The crisp mountain air was
filled with the rhythmic crunch of their snowshoes and
Avery's heavy breathing from tromping practically
straight up for the past fifteen minutes. "Also knew
the only thing that would convince you to take your
mind off work by coming here was the potential for
sexual favors."

"Already, the woman knows me well." He sent her
his most devilish smile, and she was pretty sure it was
his expression and not the cold air that made her insides quiver.

"So, where did your family go on vacation?" The
tracks of the cross-country ski course had been grooved
into the snow next to them, and they followed that
line to be sure to not get lost. A straight uphill line,

and Avery's lungs and legs sure hoped for a downhill slope soon.

"We didn't, much." He shrugged. "Both my parents are workaholic doctors, with my dad being the worst. We mostly took the occasional short trip to New York or the beach. Just for a few days, so they wouldn't be gone long."

"Ah. So you took after them?"

He flashed her a grin. "Probably. My brother, too. But I'm beginning to see the value of a little vacation time."

The path curved in a C shape to finally slope slightly downhill, thank heavens, but it was one long way down. Avery had thought she was in pretty good shape, but the burning in her thighs and lungs after the uphill climb told her maybe not so much. "Let's cut through here. Catch the path on the other side."

"I may not be a skier, but I've heard you shouldn't go off the trail. What if we fall into a crevasse?"

"You're such a rule follower. Come on."

She grabbed his hand and veered to the right near a line of trees that went all the way down the mountain.

He slid her a look that said she was crazy, but his lips were tipped into an amused smile. "There are times to follow the rules and times when it makes sense to break them. Wandering around on a mountain doesn't seem like the best time to me, but you're the tour guide. Lead on."

Even though the snow was deeper there, going downhill made it easier to breathe. And she was glad she wouldn't be panting when she asked the question she'd been wondering about. "Was there some bad situation in your life that made you not want to spend time with me after we found out who each other was? When I said it wasn't good to be involved with someone you had to work with, you were very quick to agree, and I thought there must be a reason."

"First, there was never a moment I didn't want to spend time with you. I just knew it was a bad idea." She relaxed at his teasing expression, glad he wasn't going to get all stiff again now she'd brought up the unsettling back and forth between them. "But your observation is very astute. And here I'd always heard genius types were book smart but not people smart."

She rolled her eyes. "Again, the stereotype. I thought we were done with that."

"Sorry." He took a sideways step, his shoulder bumping into hers as his eyes got that wicked glint in them. "Learning that female scientists wear lacy, colorful underwear has changed my perspective forever. Don't think I'll ever be able to see techs with their test tubes and not wonder what they have on under their lab coats."

It was utterly stupid, but his words pricked at her heart. It wasn't like they were a real couple. One that would be together after the trial was complete in just over a week. He was a career-driven man who liked women in small doses, and fantasizing about lingerie and wild sex was part of that package.

"Hey." He must have seen something in her expression because he stopped walking and tipped her chin up. "I was teasing. There's only one woman whose underwear I wonder about."

She forced a laugh. "And I just might have to keep you wondering. But you haven't answered my question."

They continued their trek as several cross-country skiers slid by in the tracks above them, and the sound of his deep sigh mingled with the swish of the skis. "When I first found out who you were I was amazed. Well, I was amazed a whole lot of ways that day." He aimed that glint at her again.

Warmth crept into her cold cheeks at his words, re-membering exactly how she'd behaved and how she'd never done such a thing in her life before. "I'd prefer you didn't remind me I slept with a man I'd just met. I'm embarrassed by that, and you know it."

"You shouldn't be." He wrapped his arm around her and tugged her close to his side. "The romance of Paris and our chemistry together made it inevitable. If it hadn't happened that day, it would have happened an-other day. From the second I turned to see the knock-out woman talking to me in the hotel, I knew it was meant to be."

His words, his low voice and the expression in his eyes caught her breath. "Maybe it was," she replied softly. "And you're still doing a darned good job of avoiding answering me."

"You just want to gloat when you hear I made a stu-pid mistake. Because you know I never do, and admit-ting I made one once isn't something I like to do."

"I know, Dr. Dunbar, that you think you're perfect."

"Hey, my mom calls me Prince Perfect. What do you expect?" That quick grin flashed again, almost as dazzling as the sunshine on the snow, and Avery had to admit he just might be as close to perfection as a man could be.

A minute went by, silent except for the crunch, crunch of their shoes, and she'd begun to think he'd never tell her when he finally spoke. "My crown slipped a few years back, though. I dated a medical supplies rep who sold, among other things, stents for angioplasty. I switched to the stent she repped because I honestly thought it might be superior to the ones I'd been using. You can imagine how many stents we use a month, and because it was more expensive, the hospital bean counters questioned it. When it came out that she and I had a personal relationship, all hell broke loose. Hospital bigwigs accused me of behaving unethically, and as it all unfolded, a whole lot of dirty laundry spilled out."

She couldn't imagine Jack having a whole lot of dirty laundry. "Like what?"

"Turned out the beguiling Vanessa was sleeping with numerous docs, in multiple hospitals, who used high-end surgical and biomedical products. She was trying to get a big promotion at her company and used me, and the other saps, to get the sales record and promotion."

He shook his head, his lips twisted into a grimace. "What a fool I was. My relationship with Vanessa was pretty much strictly physical, but knowing the truth, that she'd used me, made me feel sick. I hated answering to the ethics board, having them question my professionalism. I was cleared of any wrongdoing, but vowed I'd never so much as look at a woman involved in any way with my job."

"Wow." His story might even be worse than her former boyfriend mistakes. And explained why the wall between them had been wider even than she'd thought their situation warranted.

"Wow?" He raised his eyebrows at her. "Maybe I shouldn't have confessed. You think I'm an idiot now?"

"No, of course not. But I've gotta tell you. While I feel bad you went through that, you've made me feel a little better about my own poor judgment."

"Which would be what?"

Part of her didn't want to share something so embarrassing, but he'd shared with her, so it was only fair. "I dated a couple of cardiologists for a while. The first one traveled a lot, teaching his specialized procedures. Turned out he had a woman in every port. Or every hospital, to be more accurate."

He stopped walking to stare at her. "I can't believe there's a human alive who could be stupid enough to not hang onto you with both hands when he had the chance."

He looked genuinely astonished, and what woman wouldn't feel pretty good about his words? "The second one started talking down to me, saying disparaging things."

"What kind of disparaging things?"

"Oh, like when people asked me questions about angioplasty and stents, which happened sometimes because that's what he did, he'd say I was the 'equipment' girl and wasn't qualified to talk about medical procedures."

"You've got to be kidding me." The astonishment was still there on his face, along with anger. "No wonder you wrote off cardiologists as being total jerks. But he was probably jealous of your amazing smarts. That kind of guy isn't worth having, and you know it."

"I do know. But I guess that whole experience has made me hypersensitive. Which is why I was suspicious of you and Jessica. Sorry. But there are some real winners out there."

"Yeah. There are." His eyes and voice warmed and he stopped, turning to wrap both his arms around her and draw her close. Her own arms slipped around his back, and the sizzle between them could be felt all the way through their coats and hats, warming her from the inside out. "The kind of winner that makes a man do something he swore he wouldn't do. So maybe I'm still a fool. But I can't seem to keep you out of my head."

His cold lips touched hers, and in an instant both their mouths were toasty warm as they shared a slow, sweet kiss. Just as Avery angled her head, inviting him to delve deeper, the swishing sound of skis on snow came from above them. They pulled apart and looked up the hill to the trail they'd abandoned to see nearly a dozen skiers following one another in single file on the trail.

"Are you kidding?" Jack said. "Even out here in the middle of a mountain we have an audience?"

She wasn't about to let a few strangers ruin the heavenly moment. Of all the places she'd kissed Jack, holding him close on this wild, beautiful mountainside, his cold nose touching hers and his mouth so hot and delicious—this place was her very favorite. "Who cares? We're in France."

She tried to go up on tiptoe to kiss him again, but found it pretty difficult with snowshoes on her feet. Luckily, the superheated gleam in his eyes showed he knew exactly what she wanted and he kissed her again, sending her heart pounding even harder. Her legs wobbled, whether from the kiss or the hiking or both she wasn't sure. She hung onto Jack's coat as his mouth moved across her cold cheek and beneath her earlobe in a shivery path that made it very hard to breathe.

Frigid wind swept the cheek not currently covered by Jack's warm one and at the same time clumps of snowflakes dropped onto her face. She opened her eyes to see Jack lifting his head, a slow, sexy smile curving his lips as his finger swept the snow from her eyelashes.

"Guess we should have thought to bring your umbrella up here on the mountain with us." His hat and shoulders were covered with snowflakes, too, and she looked behind him to see the wind catch more of the snow loaded on the evergreen trees and swirl it onto them, like Mother Nature was playing a joke and tossing it with her hand.

"Who knew?"

Their steamy, breathless laughter flitted between them as they separated, her gloved hand in his, to trudge on down the mountain in a companionable silence. She pulled in a deep, satisfied breath, realizing she felt as comfortable and relaxed as she'd felt in a long, long time, and hoped Jack was feeling the same.

Except he probably wouldn't be much longer.

"So here's the other thing we have scheduled today," she said, hoping her announcement wouldn't ruin the beautiful, quiet mood between them.

"Dare I hope it's the wild sex or the wine consumption? Or both combined?"

"Not yet. That might come later, if you're good."

"Oh, I'm good. You know I'm good."

She hated to squash the teasing heat in his eyes and sucked in another breath, this one no longer relaxed. "After we turn in our snowshoes, we're going to take the car out to the Larue family vineyards."

Something in her expression obviously told him this wasn't just another pleasure excursion. "Your TAVI patient?"

"Clearly, I'm not the only astute one." Suddenly she felt nervous. Would meeting Benjamin make Jack go all defensive again? Snuff out the smile on his face, the relaxed posture, the teasing looks? Make it difficult for them to enjoy the hours together in this beautiful place?

Maybe it would. But with the complications that patients were experiencing increasing, her gut told her Jack needed to step back from how deeply he was wrapped up in the trial and think about it objectively. If meeting Benjamin didn't do that, probably nothing would. "Are you…okay with that?"

"I told you this morning, Dr. Girard," he said, his gaze steady on hers, "I'm all yours."

The house looked to be hundreds of years old, though at the same time it was still in pristine condition. Proof that most people had been shorter long ago, Jack had to duck beneath the ancient beam above the thick, wooden front door when he followed Avery, who was being kissed on both cheeks and warmly greeted by a woman who was probably in her early forties. Both were yammering on in French, and since he couldn't understand a word, he took time to look around the cozy room. A welcoming fire burned inside a huge stone fireplace, and a wooden table was covered with so many plates of finger foods you'd have thought every guest at the hotel was stopping by.

He blew out a breath. He'd known all along this was the catch to an otherwise great weekend with Avery, but now that he was here, dread began to seep into his gut. What did Avery really want from him? And what could this man have experienced that he hadn't seen before, anyway?

It wasn't as if he didn't know all too well about the challenges people with bad hearts faced every day. He stood by his statement that a less-than-perfect outcome was still better than what most had lived with before the procedure. This TAVI trial was doing important work, critical work, work that might have helped someone like his own grandfather, who had died with so much left to live for. Help a lot of people who couldn't get a new heart valve any other way.

Benjamin Larue must not have had luck on his side. Sometimes bad things happened to good people, and every doctor experienced days when it felt like a shower of bricks came down on everyone's head. When it did, it hurt like hell and left bruises that lasted a long time.

"Jack, this is Vivienne Larue. Vivienne, Dr. Jack Dunbar."

"Welcome, welcome! Please sit and make yourself comfortable while I get Benjamin. He is very happy you've come to visit."

Jack wasn't sure *visit* was the right term—why did he suddenly feel a little like he was standing in front of a firing squad? The feeling persisted, even though he sat in a comfortable chair by the flickering fire. Maybe it was the way Avery's green eyes were focused on him—*expectantly* would be the word—and that fueled his discomfort.

"So were you telling secrets about me in French?" Maybe making a joke would lighten up the awkward mood that hung like a cloud in the room.

"I don't know many of your secrets, though that one you shared on the mountain was a doozy. Can't wait to hear more and spread them all over the hospital."

Damned if the woman couldn't make him smile in the midst of an avalanche. "I might have to make up some juicy ones, just to surprise you."

"You've been surprising me since the minute we met." A sweet, sincere smile accompanied her words, and he felt himself relax a little.

"Likewise, Dr. Girard."

"Vivienne makes the best cheesy puff pastries," Avery said as she put a few things on her plate. "You should try one."

Before he could answer, he heard a sound behind him and turned to see Vivienne pushing a man in a wheelchair into the room.

It wasn't an ordinary wheelchair. It was semi-reclining, the kind someone who couldn't breathe well would use, and the man sitting in it had a prosthetic leg. His head was raised to look at his guests as introductions were made, and a friendly smile didn't mask his pallor or the thin, drawn look to his face.

So much for feeling less tense. His gut tightened all over again when he saw how young the man was to have this kind of disability. Probably only in his early forties, like his wife. It was damned unfair that sometimes a guy drew the short straw, and medical science just wasn't advanced enough to replace it with a longer one.

And wasn't that exactly why the work he was doing was so important? Advancing medical science to help patients was the critical goal.

"*Bon après-midi*, Dr. Dunbar. I'm honored to have you visit," Benjamin said in a hoarse, rasping voice as he extended his hand. "Avery tells me you have developed a new prosthetic valve device. I wish you well with it."

Jack stood and leaned over to shake his hand. "Thank you. Avery thought that speaking with you might help me do the best I can for other patients as we move forward."

Benjamin's smile broadened. "And I hope that you will taste our latest wine vintages to help me with those, as well. We make the finest wines in France right here, you know. Pinot Gris, Pinot Noir and Rieslings are our specialties."

"I didn't know. I don't pretend to be a wine expert, but I'm more than happy to lend my palate to you."

"Excellent." Benjamin beamed, then turned to talk to Avery. As Jack watched them banter, the room seemed to lose its claustrophobic feeling and he relaxed, taking a bite of the cheese Vivienne offered. Which made him realize he'd been prepared for criticism or attack or who knew what from all of them.

"So, Dr. Dunbar. Avery is determined that I tell you my story. Why she continues to take responsibility for God's hand in my life, I do not know. It is what it is. So I will recite it quickly, then we can enjoy more important things." Benjamin looked at her with an expression similar to that of a fond uncle, and her emotions were right there on her face, visible to anyone who wanted to look.

Warm friendship. Caring. Heartache and guilt.

She'd been through tough times with this man, he saw, surprised at that revelation, though he shouldn't have been. She had obviously had her own days where bricks had fallen all too hard on her head. She might not be a medical doctor, but she cared about the patients using the devices she'd designed as much as any of them. Cared about them deeply enough to forge this bond that obviously both hurt and soothed.

"I'd like to hear your story, Benjamin," he said. "More than anything, I want to help people like my late grandfather, and like you, with challenging heart valve problems."

He thought he was focused on Benjamin, but realized he was glancing at Avery, too. At her smile, and the softness in her eyes that told him she liked his response. He'd always thought he didn't care what others thought, that he worked for his patients and for the goals he'd set for himself, and that was all that mattered. But at that moment her approval brought a smile to his own face and made his chest swell a little, even though he knew that was absurd.

"At the age of nine I was diagnosed with diabetes," Benjamin said, staring at the swirl of red wine in a glass his wife had poured. "As the years went on, I was one of the less fortunate. Many complications, and eventually I lost my leg."

"Juvenile-onset diabetes can be a difficult disease to manage." Jack saw all too many patients with terrible complications from diabetes and hoped like hell researchers would eventually find a cure.

"It is." Benjamin nodded. "Then, when our boys were only seven and nine, my kidneys began to fail. We fit weekly dialysis into our schedules somehow. Along with caring for the vines and harvest and crush and all the other things that must happen for a winery to survive. For me to survive." His hand reached to Vivienne and she clasped it tight. "My beautiful wife has stood by me through all of this, and why that is I do not know. I only know that I am blessed."

"It is your stubbornness, Benjamin Larue. Your irresistible stubbornness."

Jack saw tears fill Vivienne's eyes, and he glanced at Avery to see hers had filled, as well. In her line of work she probably didn't often work with sick people. He dealt with it every day, but that didn't make it any easier. "When did you begin to have heart problems?"

"Not long after my dialysis began. When I worked with the grapes or played with my sons, I tired quickly, becoming very short of breath." His eyes met Jack's. "Do you have children, monsieur?"

"No."

"Then you do not know the joys and frustrations of their abundant energy. Energy I wanted to keep up with."

Jack might not know about wanting to play with his own children, with any children, but could easily imagine how that inability could cut away at your soul. "So you and your doctors decided a valve transplant would help. Except you weren't a candidate for open-heart surgery because of your other health issues."

"Oui. I was pleased to think a new procedure might help me breathe easier, work longer and play ball with my boys for more than five minutes." He grinned. "You may look at me and wonder, but I got pretty good at kicking with my pretend leg, which amused my children."

"Amused everyone," Avery said, smiling, too. "When his doctor and I came here to talk about the risks and benefits of the TAVI trial, I couldn't believe how Benjamin could practically do spin moves. His boys joked that he was Iron Man and had an unfair advantage. Tiring quickly was his primary problem, which we'd hoped to fix."

"But the surgery didn't go well." Jack wanted to get to the crux of the matter, though he already knew.

"Non." Benjamin's smile faded. "Afterward, I was

much worse, not better. Now if I lie flat, my lungs fill. I cannot kick the ball with my boys at all anymore or work in the vineyard. My kidney problems make it impossible for me to take a diuretic to lessen the fluid buildup, and my body is not strong enough to handle open-heart surgery." He gestured at himself. "So this is it for me. I accept it, but hurt for my family that they must do all the things in the vineyard and at home that I no longer can."

"Bottom line, Jack? It was an utter failure," Avery said, her eyes intent on his. "We wanted to make Benjamin's life better, but we made it much worse instead. I know you see patients with bad outcomes. But you've been convinced that those with leakage from the prosthetic valve are medically manageable and still better off than before. Benjamin's situation proves that's not always the case. The percentage having this problem must be very small to justify the risk."

What was he supposed to say to that? All procedures carried risks. Every single one of them, from the simplest to the most complex. But he understood the frustration and deep disappointment. Benjamin may not have had the exercise capacity he'd wanted before the procedure, but now he had none at all and couldn't even sleep in a bed with his wife.

"Papa! Papa!" Two boys careened into the room, nearly skidding to a halt next to the wheelchair, speaking fast in French until he held up his hand.

"English, please. Our guest does not speak French, and it is good for you to practice."

Both boys took a breath, and Jack was impressed at how polite they were during a brief introduction, before launching into their story again.

"*Les chevreuils* got through the fence that has a hole and into the berry bushes. They were eating up the brambles before we chased them off! Why do deer eat thorny things like that, Papa?"

"The same reason you like your mother's macaroons, I suppose."

"Are you saying that eating my macaroons is like swallowing thorns, Benjamin Larue?" Vivienne said in faux outrage, her hands fisted on her hips.

"*Non, non*, my dearest, I am saying the brambles are like a delectable delicacy to *les chevreuils*, as all your wonderful dishes are to me." His chest filled with a deep chuckle that morphed into a horrible coughing fit that immediately swept all amusement from everyone's face.

Jack tensed, wishing there was something he could do to help Benjamin breathe more easily, but there wasn't. The fluids had to work loose on their own, and he was sure everyone was as relieved as he was when the poor man's coughing finally subsided. Benjamin took a moment to catch his breath, then spoke to his sons, telling them where to get materials to repair the fence. Pride lit his eyes as they kissed both his cheeks, said their goodbyes and ran off as fast as they'd run in.

Jack thought of his own brother and how the two of them had always looked up to their dad. The man hadn't done much around the house, always busy working at the hospital. On the occasions they'd tackled a project together, though, he still remembered how he'd admired his father's smarts and physical strength. Not having that physical strength had to hurt Benjamin like hell, but thank God he still could guide and mentor his boys in other ways.

"You have a fine family, Benjamin," Jack said. "Think they'll continue the family tradition of wine making?"

"If they do not, we will disinherit them." His eyes twinkled. "Now it is time for that wine tasting, *oui*? I cannot walk down the stairs to the cellar, so we will have to enjoy it here. Vivienne, will you uncork them, *s'il vous plaît*?"

Jack saw the closeness between husband and wife just from the way they smiled at one another, and he found himself looking at Avery. Thinking about sharing that kind of lifelong bond with a woman had never been on his list of things to accomplish in his life. Wasn't sure it ever would be. But he had to admit there just might be something good about having that kind of steady love and support in good times and bad.

The Larues had managed to keep that through plenty of bad times.

Jack didn't have to know them well to hurt for them. He got why Avery wanted him to see what Benjamin lived with, but at the same time he felt she was being naive. If he counted the number of patients living less than optimal lives, he'd spend all day doing it. Life wasn't fair, that was for sure.

The clinical trial he was working so hard on was all about trying to level the playing field just a little. Trials existed for a reason, and that reason was to test new procedures and devices. If everyone threw in the towel halfway through because potential questions arose, nothing good would ever get accomplished from most of them.

Did Avery think meeting this great family that had to live with adversity and challenges would change his goals, or make him question what he wanted to accomplish? He damned well had plenty of his own patients who had to endure a life with far less than optimal physical ability. Surely she knew that.

Improving the lives of patients was all he wanted to accomplish. If she didn't understand or believe that, their time alone together this weekend wouldn't turn out the way he hoped it would.

CHAPTER THIRTEEN

SEEING THE LARUE family always left Avery with a tumble of emotions. Pleased about spending time enjoying the closeness of their family. Grateful for her own health. Sad for what they had to deal with every day. Guilt that she hadn't done a better job designing the TAVI device before it had gone to human trials.

At that exact moment she wasn't sure which emotion was winning.

Jack's arm wrapped around her waist, holding her close, might not be helping much with the guilt and sadness, but it did feel good there. Warm and comforting. Despite their height difference, their bodies seemed to fit perfectly together as they strolled through the village in search of a *biscuiterie* and the coconut macaroons Riquewihr was famous for. The shop she usually went to was closed for the winter, and she peered hopefully at dimly lit signs, trying to find another one that was open.

"There's one," Avery said, pointing down a crooked little street. "I don't remember it, but I'm sure every one of the *biscuiteries* are good."

"So you claim these cookies are the best things in the whole world?"

"The best. I guarantee you'll love them."

They went into the tiny shop and selected a few macaroons and espresso before sitting at a small table. Avery felt pretty much sapped of small talk and nibbled her cookie, hoping its deliciousness would cheer her up and make her a better companion, which she knew she couldn't claim to be at that moment.

"I have a confession to make," Jack said, looking extremely serious.

She paused with her macaroon halfway to her mouth. "A confession?"

"Yes. I'm not a big fan of coconut. In fact, I usually avoid it like flesh-eating bacteria. But if sharing coconut macaroons with you banishes the melancholy in your beautiful eyes for even a split second, I'll gladly choke one down."

As he said it, she could swear he actually shuddered, and she managed a laugh. "You believe it would cheer me up to watch you eat something you liken to flesh-eating bacteria? What does that say about the kind of person you think I am?"

"That you are caring. And that you obviously feel all beat up right now."

"There's that astute thing again."

"Don't have to be astute to see it, Avery. How you're feeling is written all over your face."

"Good to know." She closed her eyes and swallowed at the sudden lump in her throat. "I do feel beat up whenever I see them. Who wouldn't? I designed the prosthetic valve, and that valve is why his life is awful now. It's hard for me to see that wonderful family dealing with what they deal with. See Benjamin barely able to walk, when I saw him running with the boys before my TAVI device destroyed that."

"For all you know, his heart might have gotten worse anyway. The man's been dealt a bad hand of cards, and I feel for him, too." He reached for her hand, and its warmth had her holding it tight. "But if I blamed myself for every patient who didn't do well, or who died, like Henri Arnoult, I'd never be able to function and do my job. Medicine is both rewarding and damned difficult. The only way to help people is to forge on and do the best you can. Would it help people if you just stopped designing biomedical devices? Never came up with an improved stent or something no one's invented yet?"

"No. But I should have insisted it be tested further on animals first." Not that the manufacturer and sponsor would have listened anyway. "I'd hoped you'd come to see you should consider that, too, for yours."

"I am listening to you, Avery. Hearing you loud and clear, and paying attention to the reason for your worries. I want you to know that." Seeing how deeply serious and sincere he looked brought her hope that he truly meant it. "While it's impossible to know how Benjamin's health would be right now without the TAVI, I understand your point about possibly making it worse for some patients than others. This trial is already under way with patients who have no other options. I still believe we're doing far more good than harm. But since we have more than double the number of patients now giving us additional data, I will keep him in mind as we look at how things are going."

The weight in her chest lifted at the same time it squeezed even tighter. Not only did Jack respect her opinion, it sounded like this trek had accomplished her goal. How could she have thought he might be too narrow focused, too hell-bent on success, to at least listen? She'd already seen what a committed and caring doctor he was.

"Okay, for that you don't have to eat the macaroon," she said, managing a smile. "I can't believe you were going to, if you don't like coconut. Though I admit I'm incredulous that's even possible."

"Maybe I'd like it after it's touched your lips." His finger gently swiped her bottom lip and she could see bits of cookie on his finger just before he licked it off.

Had she really been yakking away with crumbs all over her mouth? Her embarrassment at that realization got shoved aside by serious body tingling at the oh-so-sensual look he was giving her.

"You know what?" He sounded genuinely surprised. "It is better. Definitely. Sweet and delectable, in fact."

"Not like flesh-eating bacteria?" She found herself staring at his mouth, and to keep herself from diving in there and tasting for herself the crumbs and espresso on his tongue, she tried for a joke. "I'm not a big fan of escargots, which I saw you gobbling up at the hotel hors d'oeuvre party. Maybe you could hold one between your lips and I'll nibble it from there. Just to see."

His laughter made her grin and realize he'd managed to squash much of the sadness she'd been feeling. Had also managed to blast away every negative thought her former relationships had stuck in her brain nearly from the first day she'd met him. Had managed to prove himself the complete package of what a sexy man should be. At that moment she knew the attraction and lust she'd felt when she'd first met him had evolved into very much more.

The thought both scared and thrilled her, and she

wasn't at all sure what to do with the realization that had just slammed her between the eyes.

"Somehow, nibbling snails from my lips doesn't sound nearly as appealing as licking cookie crumbs from yours. I think we need further research on this, Dr. Girard."

"I think we need further research on why talking about flesh-eating bacteria and nibbling snails hasn't at all dulled my desire to kiss you, Dr. Dunbar." Further research on that, and on the tender emotions swirling around her heart as she seriously considered pressing her mouth to his right then and there.

"Then I definitely want to find out what will happen if I suggest you nibble *chocolat* from my lips. Which you can bet I'm pulling from the minibar in our room the minute we get there." His voice had gone so low, his expression so wicked that her belly quivered in anticipation of any and all nibbling action.

He tossed back the last of his espresso and stood, grasping her hand and leaning down to speak close to her ear. "Bring your cookies back to the hotel so I can see how they taste licked from your lips. After I lick off the chocolate. In fact, I like the idea of keeping a database of how all kinds of things taste from your lips and other beautiful parts of your body."

Whew, boy. She felt so hot she nearly didn't bother putting on her coat before they moved out into the chilly night. Jack walked fast, and because he was holding her hand she had to nearly run to keep up.

"Slow down a little. My legs aren't as long as yours."

"Having a hard time slowing down, thinking about our future data collection." His eyes glittered in the darkness. "And I figured the pace would keep you warmer."

No need to worry about her being warm. At all. About to skirt the ornate fountain in the center of a square, she found herself, ridiculously, wanting to make a wish like she always did when she was here. She tugged his arm so he'd stop. "Let's make a wish in the fountain. I always hope it's like the Trevi Fountain in Rome."

He pulled a couple of coins from his pocket and handed one to her. "What are you going to wish for?"

"It won't come true if you tell." She looked skyward to make her wish, surprised to see how remarkably clear it was for a winter night in France, which made her think about how wonderful it would be to make love to Jack outdoors deep in the vineyards when it was warmer, which briefly sidetracked her from her mission.

She yanked her thoughts back to ponder her wish as the stars seemed to twinkle down on them. She closed her eyes and tossed the coin into the fountain with a satisfying plunk.

"Your turn."

He tossed his coin. It landed just a millimeter from hers, and she wondered if that meant something. Which was beyond silly—it was just water in a fountain, and what would she want it to mean anyway?

"Maybe you'll get lucky and your wish will come true," she said.

His expression as his eyes met hers was odd, almost serious. It was too bad it wasn't really a magic fountain, because she'd love to ask it what his wish was.

"I'm already feeling lucky. Though I very much hope I'll get even luckier."

Her insides went all quivery again, as there was no mistaking the superheated gleam that returned to his eyes as he spoke. If the two of them making love again was what he'd wished for, he'd wasted his wish. Her breath caught just looking at his handsome face and sexy smile, and she fully intended to enjoy these hours with him before the stress of work faced them once again. Before he moved on to his next trial and she went wherever her job took her.

This time, it was Avery setting the pace, giving a quick greeting to the hotel manager before running up the two flights of stairs to their floor and into the room.

"For some reason, I'm feeling a little déjà vu," Jack said as he shoved the door closed behind them. "If it was summertime, I'd be sneaking into one of the vine-yards and feeding you grapes while making love to you under the stars."

Did the man have mind-reading powers, too, or was it just part of this electric connection they seemed to have? "Funny, I was just thinking the same thing. We could add grapes to the database." Breathlessly, she wrangled off her coat and tossed it on the chair. "It does seem like we've done the same dash into a hotel room several times since we met, wearing an awful lot of heavy clothes."

"Not exactly the same dash. For one thing, it seemed like you weren't too sure you wanted to unbutton your coat before. This time you're ahead of me." He reached for her and pulled her close. "Not to mention that, each time, it's gotten even sweeter. I'm betting tonight will be also, not even counting the macaroons you brought."

"Know what? You do taste sweeter than any cookie." She stood on tiptoe and slid her hands behind his head before she kissed him. Deeply, deliciously, pouring herself into it, wanting to show him how much she'd come to care for him. To tell him without words how impressed she was that he'd shared his honest view about Benjamin and medicine, while still listening to her, respecting her, caring what she thought. To enjoy the connection they shared that was of both mind and body.

He kissed her back. And kissed her. Until her breath was choppy and her knees nearly stopped holding her up. Figuring she'd like to be sitting or something before that happened, she backed them both toward the bed, but he stopped the movement and broke the kiss. He stood there just staring at her with eyes that were peculiarly serious behind the obvious desire shining there.

"What?" she whispered.

"When I came to Paris I was keyed up and couldn't think about anything but how all my work was about to pay off. Being with you that first day seemed like a great way to take the edge off before the trial started." He slowly shook his head. "But it didn't quite work out that way. Instead, you've added another edge."

"What do you mean?"

"I hate not having complete control over how I feel about you." He pressed her body so close to his it was hard to breathe. "I've spent my adulthood being in control of my life and my career. Not having that makes me damned uncomfortable."

Her heart constricted into a cold little ball at the fact that she was the one who had control over this current phase of his career that was so important to him. And he'd be very angry and upset that she hadn't shared that reality with him, if he ended up finding out. Or if she had to wield that control and power.

And yet somehow her heart swelled, too, at his words and the way he looked at her. Like she'd come to mean as much to him as he had to her. "Is being in control all the time important? Because right now I wouldn't mind you losing control a little."

"Yeah?" She thought he was about to resume their motion toward the bed, but he veered sideways toward the bathroom. At the same time he somehow managed to slip her blouse over her head, unzip the back of her skirt, yank off his own shirt and pants, and throw a condom onto the floor until they were standing naked just outside the tiny shower.

"I've heard the verse 'Jack, be nimble, Jack, be quick,'" she said, amazed and more than excited as she stared at his all-too-sexy physique. "Was that written about you?"

"You make me want to be quick. For some things, not everything." His lips curved. "Not jumping over any candlesticks, though. Wouldn't stay lit for what I'm planning next."

"And what are you planning next?" Avery quivered at the superheated gleam in his eyes, knowing whatever it was would be a whole lot better than any snail nibbling.

Jack turned the faucet on, then tugged Avery's breathtakingly naked body into the cubicle and closed the door.

"My plan is to lick water from every inch of your skin," he said. The closeness of the space sent her pink nipples nudging against his chest and his erection into the softness of her belly, making him groan. Still-cold water rained onto his back as he shielded her from it until it warmed, but it didn't do a thing to cool the heat pumping through every one of his pores.

"It's small in here, I know. But I don't care. I liked kissing the rainwater from your face and mouth so much I've been fantasizing about getting you in the shower ever since."

"Should I get my umbrella? I kind of liked kissing you under that before we got all wet."

"Maybe next time." God, she was adorable. "I'm already all wet, and soon you will be, too."

He kissed her, letting one hand palm her breast while the other stroked down her soft skin and between her legs to make his last statement come true. The little gasping breaths and sexy sounds coming from her mouth into his nearly had him diving into her right then and there, but tonight was about slow and easy. Being together just this once without work and patients and the trial hanging around with them.

The water pounding on his back had finally warmed, and he pulled her under it to join him. He shoved her wet hair back so he could see her beautiful face and started with her forehead, sipping the water from her skin as it tracked down her cheek, her throat, her breasts.

Her fingers dug into his back as he tasted as much of her as her could reach, and the feel of her tongue licking across his shoulder, too, up his neck and around his ear, made him shiver and burn at the same time.

"You taste so delicious," he murmured against her damp sternum as her other slick wetness soaked his fingers and the scent of her touched his nose, making him want to taste her there, too. Probably not possible in the tiny shower, but later? Oh, yeah. "The best dessert any man could ask for."

"This water doesn't taste as good as the rain, though." Her chest rose and fell against his mouth. "Maybe we should try bottled water, since I don't think they drink tap water here."

"Too late for that." He chuckled and looked up at her, then paused in mid-lick. Arrested by the look on her face. It was filled with the kind of intimate connection between them he'd only felt with her—a humor and euphoria and something he couldn't quite define. He wanted to see more of it, wanted to look into her eyes as he kissed her mouth. Every bit of her tasted beyond wonderful, but that delectable mouth of hers was his absolute favorite of all.

Grasping her rear in his hands, he wrapped her legs around his waist, then realized he had to get the condom from the floor. He crouched down, juggling her on his knees as he reached for it, but she slid sideways. Mashing her close against him so she wouldn't crack her head on the tile wall, he fell back on his tailbone, his erection nearly finding home base as she slid forward on top of him.

"Well, hell. Note to self. Even the best idea can be ruined by poor planning." He steadied them both, resisting the urge to massage his sore butt, and saw she was stifling a laugh.

"NOT RUINED. ALTERED." She grabbed the trouble-making condom and tore the wrapper, and he thought he might come unglued as she opened it and rolled it on, then slowly eased herself onto him.

"Is this a good alteration to the plan?" she asked in a sultry voice as she moved on him, her eyes all smoky green, her beautiful lips parted, and he had to try twice before he could manage a short answer.

"Yes. Good." The back of his head was against the hard tile wall, his neck all kinked, and he was practically folded into a pretzel as the water still flowed and pooled on the shower floor, but none of that mattered.

All he could feel was her heat wrapped around him. All he could see was the vision that was her—her breasts, her hips, her face, the total goddess that was Avery Girard. He reached up to touch all of it, all of her, pulling her to him for the deepest kiss of his life as she increased the pace. As he felt her orgasm around him and followed her there.

Warm and bonelessly relaxed, Jack held Avery close beneath the sheets and down blanket. Round two in bed with the promised *chocolat* from the minibar had been every bit as good as the shower, which he'd never have believed until he'd experienced it.

"You were right, you know," he murmured against her silky hair.

"I usually am." He could feel her lips curve against his arm, and he smiled, as well. "What was I right about this time?"

"I did need a break. I needed to relax so I have a clear mind when I get back to work tomorrow. So thank you for that."

"Thank you for coming to meet Benjamin and listening to my worries with an open mind. That's all I wanted."

"All you wanted? Not me licking water and chocolate from you?"

"Okay, I wanted that, too."

He loved that little gleam in her eye and got distracted for a few minutes from something he'd been wanting to ask, having to kiss her again. When he finally came up for air he slipped her hair from her eyes and refocused his attention from the libido that kept leaping onto center stage around her.

"I've been wondering why you haven't come up with a next-generation TAVI device," he said. "You had to have heard through the biomedical grapevine I was working with Crilex on one. Is it because of Benjamin?"

"No. I can't quit trying to come up with a design to help people like him. I have a couple I'm working on. But I want the most promising device to be tested on animals until we're as sure as we can be of a positive outcome for patients. If I let a trial get started too soon, it's out of my hands after that."

"You didn't have much say during your first one?"

"No. Even after the percentage of patients with aortic insufficiency was too high and then Benjamin had his catastrophic problem, the sponsor insisted on finishing the trial."

Finally, he got why she wasn't working for that company anymore, doing freelance work instead. "So you quit."

"I quit. I know trials carry risks, and patients know those risks. But for the cardiologist and corporation to ignore them when things have obviously gone wrong? That's unacceptable."

"And you think that's what I'm doing?"

"No." Her lips pressed softly against his arm, and he pulled her closer against him, glad that was her answer. "I don't think this trial is there yet. But it might get there, and if it does, I hope you'll do the right thing and shut it down."

"I want to finish the trial and study the data for the rollout, because I think we have to do that to come to any real conclusion." He hoped she understood his perspective. "If there was an extreme and obvious high risk, though, I wouldn't put patients' lives in harm's way to accomplish that."

"I know that now." Her teeth gleamed white in the low light. "That's why I'm lying here in bed with you, sticky with chocolate."

"Happy to lick you more to clean it off, if you like."

"Need to record the current data first. Macaroons, wine, espresso, chocolate." She pushed up onto her elbow. Her soft hand stroked across his chest, and he captured it in his, kissing her fingers and sucking the chocolate still clinging to one until she laughed and yanked it free. "So, you know my dirty little secret about the failure of my device and the failure of the people in charge to abort the mission. Tell me how you became so passionate about a second TAVI device."

He sighed. The subject of his grandfather still had the power to bring an ache to his chest. So much knowledge and grace had died with the man.

"My dad, my brother and I all decided to become cardiologists because of my granddad. I wish you could have met him—he was just a great guy and a great doc. Always seemed ironic that he had a heart attack when he was only in his fifties and suffered for years from a faulty valve afterward. He eventually had open-heart surgery, but he was one of the small percentage who didn't make it through."

"I'm sorry, Jack."

Her hand slipped up his chest to cup his cheek, and he liked the feel of it there. He turned his face to kiss her palm. "The more I worked with various stents in interventional cardiology, the more convinced I got that we could solve that problem. Help patients without other

options and someday have the TAVI procedure completely eliminate the need to perform open-heart surgery for valve replacement. I want that to happen. And
I want to be a part of it."

"You already are. No matter how things end up, this
step you've taken is a huge one. Mine was, as well. Un-
successful, yes, but each time, no matter what, we learn
something that will help us do it better next time."

"Is that the biomedical engineering creed?" While
he admired the hell out of her attitude, and agreed with
it, he couldn't help teasing her a little, wanting to bring
a smile back to her now somber face.

"My creed. Yours, too, I bet."

"Yeah. Mine, too." He wasn't even close to giving up
on this device. He was still convinced, even if Avery
wasn't, that rolling it out to other hospitals remained
the ultimate way to study it.

CHAPTER FOURTEEN

"Aʜ, Dʀ. Dᴜɴʙᴀʀ, you will promise I can tend my garden after you fix me, *oui*?"

"No promises, Mrs. Halbert. But I'll do the best I can. What do you like to grow in your garden?"

The smile Jack was giving the woman, the way his eyes crinkled at the corners and how he seemed genuinely interested in her garden all made Avery's heart feel squishy. It wasn't the first time that organ had felt that way around him. In fact, he'd made it squish a little their very first day together, and it had gotten to the point where it became pretty much a melted mess whenever he was around.

That she'd ever believed the success of this trial was important to him for his personal fame and fortune—more important than the success of the patients' health—made her cringe now. It was so obvious he was doing this to help people with no other surgical option. To someday change valve replacement surgery altogether, as she had wanted to do. To honor the memory of his beloved grandfather.

"I know I cannot dig my leeks from the ground. But grow chard and cucumbers, *oui*? My grandchildren love it when I fix them. And to prune my roses. *Est-ce que je serai capable de la faire?*"

He glanced at Avery, and she quickly translated. "She wants to know if she'll be able to do that after the surgery."

Jack placed his hand on the woman's gnarled one. "I hope so, Mrs. Halbert. Maybe I'll be here when you come for checkups this summer. I'd like it if you would bring me one of the roses you've pruned, to see and smell what you love to grow."

"Oui, oui." The woman beamed and patted his hand resting on hers. *"Quelle couleur? Rose? Blanche? Rouge?"*

Avery was about to translate again, but he was obviously able to figure it out as he smiled first at the woman, then at her in a slow perusal from head to toe. "I'm fond of every color, Mrs. Halbert. Preferably enjoyed all at once."

As his eyes met hers, that squishy feeling rolled all around in her belly. When he turned back to the patient she glanced down at herself and the yellow blouse and red shoes she wore. She decided she just might have to buy a new scarf in multiple hues to go with them for the next time she and Jack went out together.

The thought surprised her. Since when had she ever dressed for anyone but herself? Apparently the answer was, *not until she'd met Jack.*

Nurses came in to prep Mrs. Halbert for surgery, and as Jack spoke with them Avery quietly left the room. She pulled up the data from the past three days of surgery after she and Jack had returned from their weekend together. The weekend that had left her with the unsettling yet exhilarating knowledge that, for good or bad, her heart was in Jack's hands.

She hadn't planned on falling for him. For anybody. And she was pretty sure Jack was in the same boat. But since it was too late to keep it from happening, she fully intended to see just where these new feelings she hoped he shared might take them.

Yet there was that one potentially huge, very worrying issue with that, and she felt a little queasy just thinking about it. More than a little queasy, as she studied the information she'd gathered onto her tablet.

The dramatically increased patient load in the trial and the resulting data had waving red caution flags written all over it. If it continued like this, she would have to try to convince Jack to halt the trial. If that couldn't be accomplished, she'd have no choice at that time but to recommend to Bob it be halted and that future trials be discontinued.

Her stomach churned more, even as she hoped against hope that things would improve with the surgeries scheduled over the next couple of days. But if they didn't, if that's what had to happen, would Jack understand and agree?

She didn't know. But one thing she did know. No matter how much she'd come to care for him, those feelings would not get in the way of her professional integrity.

"Breathing better now, Mrs. Halbert?" Jack asked. It felt like he'd said those words a dozen times in just the past eight days, and it took a major effort to keep his voice calm and steady when he wanted to slam his fist into the wall and kick something.

"Oui. Better."

This déjà vu wasn't the great kind he'd shared with Avery, running to hotel rooms together. This was a recurring nightmare for both his patients and himself.

After taking the weekend off with Avery, Jack had returned to work feeling ready to take on the world. That feeling of energy and optimism had been quickly replaced by stress and anxiety as no fewer than three patients from last week and two from this one were already suffering with leakage from their new valves.

He studied Mrs. Halbert, very glad to see that her hands had loosened their grip on her chest and each inhalation seemed more even and less labored. He checked her vitals, asked the nurse to look at the fluid in her Foley and listened to her lungs, which were definitely clearer. Blood pressure improved, oxygen improved. Crisis hopefully over, and she'd be okay.

"Sorry you got that scare." He reached for her hand. "I know it feels bad when you can't catch your breath. But I believe you're going to feel pretty good by the time you go home to prune those roses."

"Merci beaucoup." She gently patted his hand as she'd done every time he'd talked with her. If the woman had been in an advertisement playing a dear, lovely grandma, people would have bought whatever she was selling, and his chest felt a little heavy as he wondered if the sweet woman would be thanking him in a few months.

Think positively. He checked her pulse again and reminded himself she'd likely do just fine with meds to control the leakage, which was thankfully minor. But as he looked at the smile on her wrinkled face he saw someone younger. Benjamin Larue, who couldn't

even sit upright without drowning in the fluid that collected in his lungs.

"I'll be back to check on you later, Mrs. Halbert." He
shoved to his feet, spoke again to the nurse and said his
goodbyes. Then saw Avery standing in the doorway.

Her expression bore no resemblance at all to the flirtatious, fun Avery he'd spent the weekend with. The
woman looking at him rivaled a grimly stern princi-
pal about to haul a student off to her office, and Jack
braced himself for the lecture she'd given before that he
absolutely did not want to hear again at that moment.

He walked past her into the hallway, and she followed. He closed his eyes for a moment, trying to find
his calm, before he turned to her and held up his hand.
Needing to stop whatever she was about to say before
it started, because it had been a damn long day and
week and he knew his nerves were worn thin enough
that he just might say something he regretted. He liked
her—hell, more than liked her—and respected her, and
getting into an argument with her was the last thing he
wanted to do.

"I know the percentage of patients with problems is
higher than we expected," he said. "I know you're worried that some won't be medically manageable, and I
know you think we should perform the procedure on
fewer patients as we finish the trial. I know, Avery."

"So what are you going to do about it?"

What *was* he going to do about it? Very good question, and one he didn't have a clue how to answer. He
scrubbed a hand over his face, and when he looked at
her again, saw her beautiful green eyes were somehow
both soft and hard as they met his.

"Last week I was worried, but still watching. This

week, in just ten surgeries, you've had two major leak-ages, and now Mrs. Halbert, which makes it thirty per-cent. Sweet Mrs. Halbert, who just wants to be able to prune her roses." She shook her head. "I think you know what you should do. The real question is whether or not you will."

"First, Mrs. Halbert's original valve was so diseased she could barely walk twenty steps. Second, thirty per-cent of patients in three days isn't thirty percent over the entire trial, which you may not be aware is how data must be collected."

Her mouth dropped open. "That's a nice insult. Re-minds me of another cardiologist I used to be involved with."

Damn it. "I'm sorry, that was just frustration talking. You know I admire and respect you and your expertise." The disappointment he saw in her eyes made him want to punch himself the way he'd wanted to punch the wall. Saying something he shouldn't was exactly why he'd wanted to avoid the whole conversation. "But you think it's black and white. It isn't. If we reduce the number of patients, there might be fewer with problems, but there will also be fewer who get the help they need. Some who might die soon because their aortic valve barely works. Have you taken the time to talk to any of them or their families? Because I have."

He knew his voice was rising, and he sucked in a breath to control it, walking farther down the hall away from the rooms. He turned to her again, and she had that damned tablet clutched to her breast like a shield. "I've told them exactly how the trial is going, good and bad, and asked if they still wanted to participate. And you know what? They do. For almost all of them this

is their last shot at a decent life. Or life at all. We won't
have the conclusive data we need until trials are conducted over the next year at various hospitals."

"The data is screaming at you, Jack, but you're not
listening."

"I am listening. I'm hearing the patients talk and the
data talk. After it's rolled out everywhere it's scheduled to be, we'll listen to the entire conversation and go
from there." He dropped a quick kiss on her forehead,
knowing even that connection would ease his frustration with her and the situation. "I've got to get to my
next surgery."

He scrubbed, then headed to the cath lab, working hard
to bring his focus where it needed to be. Jessica was
already there, arranging the last items needed for surgery, and she handed him his lead apron.

"Can I talk to you privately for a minute before surgery gets started?" she asked, glancing around at the
doctors and nurses starting to filter in behind the glass
wall in the cath lab to observe. Then she focused a laser
look at Jack that was odd enough to grab his attention.
He nearly asked why before just giving her a nod and
moving to a quiet corner where he didn't think anyone
would be able to hear them.

"What's up?"

"I found out something this morning that you're not
going to like." Jessica's lips were pressed into a tight
line and a deep frown had formed between her brows.
In the three years they'd worked together she hadn't
been a woman prone to drama. Big drama was written
on her face now, though, and he felt a little fissure of
concern slide down his spine.

"This sounds ominous. We're getting started soon, so make it fast, please."

She glanced behind them again before speaking, keeping her voice low. "I was in the back room finishing up some things after your last surgery yesterday evening. Bob Timkin was there, talking to a hospital administrator type from a different French hospital who had just arrived in Paris to observe the trial. Timkin was showing him the TAVI device and talking it up. But when the guy asked him about conducting a trial at his hospital in Nice, I was surprised when Timkin put him off. Said we had to finish this trial first and see what the results were before they considered any rollout."

Jack frowned. "That can't be what he said. The whole reason French interventional cardiologists have been here observing how the procedure is done is so they can conduct their own trials. The trials at other French hospitals are about ready to begin."

"How long have we worked together, Jack?" Jess fisted her hands on her hips. "I heard him say it with my own ears. Are you implying I'm confused?"

"I believe you heard something. But it just doesn't make sense, so I have to think you missed some important part of the conversation." He trusted that Jessica must have heard a conversation that had been out of the ordinary. But it didn't add up. "Crilex has poured money into the development of the device and this trial for that exact reason—to conduct additional trials elsewhere for the next year. We've just begun to collect the data."

"I know. But, believe me, I didn't misunderstand. So, when he left to take the guy to dinner, I was glad he left his Crilex binders behind. He must have gotten them later, though, because this morning they were gone."

"You were planning to snoop through them?" Jack nearly smiled despite concerns about this conversation they were having. Jessica was the queen of snooping into things around the hospital she ordinarily wouldn't be privy to. "Must have ruined your morning that they were gone."

"A little." A small, return smile flitted across her face before that deeply serious expression came back. "But I did get a chance to snoop through them some. Quite a bit, actually, until a couple of people came in. Enough to surprise and worry me. I didn't call you about it then, because I'd hoped to look more this morning, to make sure I wasn't reading it wrong. So here's the other part you're not going to like."

Her expression was so dark and downright grim his chest tightened and the alarm bells rang louder in his brain. "Spill it, Jess. We don't have all day."

"Genius biomedical engineer Dr. Girard isn't here to just observe and possibly use ideas from this device on a new one she might design in the future. Crilex hired her to give her evaluation of your device regarding its safety and effectiveness. At the end of the thirty days, if she gives them the green light, they'll roll out the trials elsewhere. If she doesn't, Crilex won't fund any more clinical trials with it."

Jack stared at her in utter disbelief. "There's no way you can be right about that. No one can make any kind of final judgment call on a device's success or failure after just one month of clinical trials. That's ridiculous."

"It may be ridiculous, but I'm telling you it's true. And there's more." She stepped even closer, speaking in a conspiratorial whisper. "I wanted to make sure you knew before the procedures today, so you could watch your back and be careful what you say and do. Here at the hospital and before you get in any deeper with her."

The numb shock he was feeling started to take over his whole body. "Make sure I knew what?"

"The whole reason Dr. Girard is here is because she approached Crilex after seeing, in all the medical journals, details on the new design for the upcoming trials. And articles about you, working together with bioengineers to develop it. She told them, just like she told you, that she believes your design hasn't fixed the valve leakage problem hers had. Crilex decided they should listen. They don't want to pour millions more into something if it has an obvious defect. They'd rather put that money into a new design, then conduct trials with that one. I don't know about you, but I'm thinking she'd rather design her own for them, which is why she's 'concerned' about yours."

The numbness faded, morphing into a hot, burning anger. Could any of this possibly be true? That, all along, Avery had withheld from him the fact that she had full control of the future of this trial? That she'd told the product developer and sponsor of these trials she thought the device he'd worked on for over a year was bad?

He sucked in a calming breath. Jessica hadn't had time to read through all the binders. Maybe she was wrong. Maybe there was a mistake.

One thing was certain, though. After this procedure, he was damned well going to find out.

Avery stood in Bob Timkin's office, waiting for him and Jack. After the last surgery, Jack had asked her to meet them here in such a tense voice she wondered if he might be coming around to her suggestion to halt the trial.

Except when he walked into the room her stomach clenched when she saw the hard look on his face. It didn't seem to be a "you might be right" expression, but who knew?

He folded his arms across his chest and stared at her. "I've been trying to figure out how to ease into this, but I'm just going to ask. Did you go to Crilex with your concerns that I thought you'd only shared with me about the new TAVI device? And did they then hire you to evaluate the device and give your opinion on its safety and effectiveness? To decide if more trials should be conducted or not?"

Avery felt like she'd swallowed the big bomb he'd just dropped. How had he found out? And what should she say? She was contractually bound to secrecy on the subject.

"I've been here to observe the new device and the clinical trial. You know that." Which was true. Just not all of it.

"Cut the crap, Avery." Anger flared in his eyes. "I may have only known you a few weeks, but I can tell when you're lying. So tell me the damned truth. I think you owe me that."

"I like you a lot, Jack, and I respect you and the work you do. But I don't owe you anything." She breathed deeply before forging on. "The people I owe are the patients who went through the trial with my first device. People like Benjamin Larue. The people I owe are the patients going through this trial now."

"So it is true," he said in a rough, disbelieving voice. He shoved his hand through his hair. Stared at her like

he was seeing her for the first time. "So you get to decide if it works or if it doesn't? If it's worth putting
money into the next trials? That while you've feigned
interest in how I think it's all going, you haven't really
given a damn because you're calling the shots?"

Her hands felt icy cold and she rubbed them together.
Wrung them, really, before she realized what she was
doing and flattened them against her stomach. "Yes."
She braced herself for whatever reaction he was going
to have to what she had to say. "After I voiced my concerns Crilex management decided that if patients have
significant problems during this trial, it might make
more financial sense to put their money into a next-
generation device. They don't want to spend millions
on multiple and extended clinical trials only to have to
redesign the device and start all over again."

"You know damned well that this trial, even with the
increased patient load, won't provide close to enough
data to make any kind of final judgment." The anger
rolling from him now was nearly palpable. "Who do
you think you are? Just because you designed the first
device, it doesn't make you qualified to make that kind
of call on a procedure like this. You're not the cardiologist doing detailed study of the patients' history. You're
not the doctor performing surgery on the patients, taking their vital signs and carefully monitoring them post-
op. Taking notes from the charts the *doctor* has written
isn't even close to the same thing as medically caring
for them."

Her own anger welled in her chest. Here it was. The
same kind of insult her old boyfriend had liked to give
her—that she'd been so sure Jack would never throw
at her. "I may not be a cardiologist or a medical doc-

tor but, believe me, I am more than qualified to know whether the device is safe or not and effective or not."

His eyes narrowed at her. "This whole thing smacks of unethical self-interest to me. You collect data on the trial, tell them the device is flawed and the roll-out should be stopped, and suddenly Crilex hires you to design the new one. No more messing around doing freelance work. You'll have a nice steady job and pay-check for a long while."

"That's beyond insulting." How had she thought he might be different from other egotistical, jerky cardi-ologists? "I have no expectation of being hired by Cri-lex. They have a great team of bioengineers, which you know very well since you worked with them to get this catheter designed. I resent you questioning my ethics and integrity."

"And I resent that you kissed up to me. Now I know why you approached me in the hotel and invited me out for the day, ending up in bed. You knew who I was and hoped I'd let slip some concerns of my own about the device or trial that you could use against me." He pointed his finger at her. "Stay out of my cath lab, Avery."

"For the record, I had no idea who you were. But it doesn't matter. You may be the brains and brawn behind this trial, Jack, but Crilex is the sponsor, which means they're running this show, not you. And they have given me authority to decide the next act."

Jack's heart was pounding so hard he thought it might burst from his chest. He'd thought the déjà vu with Mrs. Halbert had been unpleasant? This reenactment of the way Vanessa had used him to advance her career stunned him. Avery had pretended to like him when, in reality, she'd used him and the situation to snatch the reins of the trial from him, design a new catheter and run with it in her deceiving little hands.

"Doctors." Timkin came into the room to stand between them, frowning. "What's the disagreement here?"

"I've just discovered you gave her the authority to evaluate this TAVI device. Behind my back, keeping me in the dark. I've worked almost two years on this damned project, but you leave its future to someone else?"

"Jack. We simply wanted her expertise to contribute to the data collection. While it's true we asked her to give her opinion at the end of the trial, we have always fully expected there to be a full rollout when it's complete."

"Why didn't you tell me?" He wouldn't have let himself get so wrapped up in her if he'd known. He found himself looking at her beautiful, lying face, and wanted to kick himself. Wrapped up in her? Damn it, he felt so entwined with Avery he knew the pain of all this would twist him in knots for years to come.

"It seemed best to not have you distracted by any concerns about the future trials. You had enough on your plate getting everything set up for this one."

"I think you deemed it best for *you* not to have me go off on you. I don't appreciate my sponsor not being up-front with me, hiring someone to collect data behind my back and report to you."

"You knew I was collecting data for the study, which I've encouraged you to look at, so don't accuse me of doing it behind your back," Avery said, her eyes flashing green sparks. "Except you haven't wanted to really look at it."

"Tell me this." He turned to Timkin. "If Dr. Girard claims the device is unsafe, will Crilex hire her to design the next-generation one?"

"I already told you," Avery said hotly, "that Crilex's own biomedical engineers—"

"Yes," Timkin interrupted. "We would offer that position to Dr. Girard, should that be the case."

Jack could hardly breathe. He'd known it and had to believe she'd known it, too. "Funny, these self-interested concerns of yours, that you said you wanted to be 'honest' with me about. What a joke."

"My concern now is that thirty percent of patients have had serious to mild valve leakage just this week," she said. "Fourteen percent overall so far, which is more than double the expected number. The trial should be stopped and the data analyzed before any more procedures are performed."

"How do you feel about that, Jack?" Timkin asked.

How did he feel about her deception and the way she'd used him and her wanting to stop the trial right now so she could get started in her new, cushy job? Shocked and furious barely covered it. "It's a normal risk. All patients are being medically managed, and we've barely begun to have any kind of big picture here. You've already invested a lot in this device, and we need the year's worth of data," he said to Timkin. "Are you going to listen to her or to me?"

"Both. We'll decide on the rollout after everyone in this trial has received the TAVI. I need sufficient data to give shareholders as we decide to fund either this device or the next one."

"Now, there's some impressive corporate talk. Numbers instead of lives." Avery stared at them both, slowly shaking her head. "You told me, Jack, that you wouldn't put patients in harm's way if the risk became obvious."

"I said extreme risk. Fourteen percent isn't extreme."

She didn't rebut his statement, simply looking at him like he'd disappointed her ten times as much as her past boyfriends combined.

He told himself he didn't care. She'd used him and lied to him. He'd screwed up big time, believing in her, but that was over with. "Is this meeting done? I have work to do."

Slowly and carefully, she held the tablet out to him. "Good luck and goodbye. I can't be a part of something I no longer believe in."

She was quitting? Jack couldn't analyze the burning sensation in his gut, but he wasn't sure it was relief.

He watched the sway of her hips as she walked away, hating that he still wanted to. Watched as she moved all the way to the end of the hall and out the door, because he knew it was the last time he'd get to enjoy the view he never should have enjoyed to begin with.

He squared his shoulders. Work was what he did and who he was—always had been. It was past time to remember that.

CHAPTER FIFTEEN

AVERY WANDERED THROUGH Montmartre on her way to the apartment she'd been lucky enough to find available to rent for a few months.

She'd always loved this neighborhood. Loved walking the cobbled streets, window shopping in all the art stores and seeing the Sacré Coeur, which was beautiful any time of day.

Today, though, her soul wasn't filled with the pleasure of it all, bringing a smile to her face. Instead, it felt hollow and empty, because all she could think about was Jack. How angry and shocked he'd been, as she'd known he would be. How obviously beyond disappointed in her that she'd kept the secret she'd been asked to keep. Maybe she should have handled it differently somehow, but it was too late now.

There was plenty of disappointment to go around. She just didn't understand him. How could he be so blind to the fact that there were simply too many patients having problems to go on with business as usual?

She knew he was an excellent, caring doctor. An incredible man. But it seemed he cared more for his career and the future of the trial than he did for his patients.

Or maybe his determination and narrow focus was keeping him unrealistically optimistic when it was clearly time to look at everything more objectively.

Out of the corner of her eye she saw a couple kissing and realized she was standing at the Wall of I Love You. It was the day before Valentine's Day, which hadn't been her favorite holiday anyway, but now was a day she wished would forever disappear from the calendar.

Her heart ached, thinking of being here in Montmartre with Jack. Thinking of their time together all over Paris, and in Riquewihr, and how much she'd come to care for him.

How she'd come to fall in love with him.

Her throat clogged, and she sniffed and swallowed hard, quickly moving away from the wall. There'd be no reunion with Jack, here or anywhere. The universe had gotten it wrong somehow, and it just wasn't meant to be between them the way she'd come to think maybe it was.

Time to get back to her computer and back to work on a new TAVI device that maybe some company would want to fund. And tomorrow, on Valentine's Day?

Tomorrow she'd load up on tissues and romantic movies and marshmallows and coconut macaroons, giving herself a whole day to cry.

Jack stared at the X-ray fluoroscopy as he seated the prosthetic valve into the patient's heart, surprised and none too happy that in the midst of it a thought of Avery flashed through his mind. The thought that he wished she was watching. That she could see she'd been wrong to quit. Wrong to want to shut down the trial since, so far, not a single one of the last eight patients had had any problems with their new valves.

He told himself it didn't matter whether she was there or not. That he should be glad. But he couldn't deny that, without her behind that glass wall, the cath lab felt empty. The air flat and dull. The woman brought an effervescence and energy everywhere she went, and even though he hated that he did, he missed it.

"Valve looks like it's fully in place and seating nicely, so I'm withdrawing the catheter and guide wires," he said to those watching. There were some new docs there today from outside France, interested in bringing a trial to their own hospitals, and he was damned glad things were finally going more smoothly.

Except, suddenly, they weren't. The wire wouldn't release from the valve the way it was supposed to. With a frown, he gently pushed, pulled, and twisted it, but it was stuck like a damn fish hook in rocks on a riverbank.

"Get the patient's feet up in the air to see if a change in position helps the wire release."

Jessica did what he asked, and he worked at it a few more minutes, but nothing. "Try helping him roll onto his right side. If that doesn't work, roll him to the other side." More minutes, more tugging and jiggling, more nothing.

Damn it to hell. "Jess, grab my cellphone and get Toby Franklin on the line. The bioengineer from Crilex who helped design the device. Quick."

Jess hurried to make the call, explained the problem, then held the phone to Jack's ear.

"Toby. I've been trying for ten minutes to get the guide wires loose. Any ideas?"

"Put the patient in the left lateral decubitus position," Toby said. "See if having him take a deep breath to increase the pressure in his chest cavity helps. Then give it a good twist to the left, pull, and pray like hell."

Sweating now, Jack did what Toby had suggested and nearly shouted *Hallelujah!* when the wires finally released from the valve and he was able to slowly withdraw them. "Okay. We're almost done. Get ready to clamp the artery so I can close the access site."

He dragged in a deep, relieved breath as Jessica and the other nurse put a weight on the artery in the man's leg, then clamped it. Able to take a brief break, the thought of Avery flashed into his brain again. This time he realized he was glad she hadn't been there to see the problem, though he shouldn't feel that way. He couldn't take every damned thing that went wrong as a personal failure. But the fact that it had happened at all would suggest a design flaw different than any they'd seen so far. He didn't want to talk about it with her, but definitely planned to discuss it with Toby.

"Dr. Dunbar, patient's pressure is dropping."

He looked up from closing the access site in the man's leg to see Jessica frowning at the monitors. "What is it?"

"Was one twenty. Now it's one hundred—no, ninety—and his pulse is dropping." Her eyes were wide with concern as she looked at him over her mask. "Oxygen saturation is falling, too."

What the hell? "Give him a liter of fluid and get an echo."

Jessica quickly rolled over the echo machine and got a picture. Jack stared at the image of the man's heart. The valve looked snugged in right where it belonged.

He peered closer and his own heart practically stopped when he saw the one thing he dreaded to see.

"Oh, no," Jessica whispered. Obviously, she'd seen it, too, and they stared together for a split second before Jack snapped himself back into action.

"We have a large, pericardial infusion," he announced to the room, his throat tight. "Jess, page Anton Maran. He's the thoracic surgeon on call. Somebody get in touch with Anesthesia. Everybody move to get the patient to the OR fast. We don't have a single second to spare."

The room became a flurry of activity as they got the patient ready, running down the hall with Jack as he pushed the gurney, because saving the man's life would require fast work and a lot of luck.

Breathing hard, his mind spun back to the whole procedure. How could he possibly have perforated the man's ventricle? There was just one, obvious answer. Somehow, when he'd had to twist and pull the wires to get them to release from the valve, the catheter had torn it.

"Is he going to make it?" Jessica asked as she ran along beside him.

"Stitching the cut will be easy for Anton. Getting him to the OR on time will be the hard part. The other part of the whole equation is whether or not he can recover from the open-heart surgery we were trying to avoid."

Jack said a prayer of thanks that Anton Maran and the anesthesiologist were already scrubbed up and in the OR when they wheeled the patient in. He briefed Anton, but they'd already spent time going over each patient just in case there was an emergency like this one, so he was able to get to work fast.

Jack watched throughout the whole procedure. The shock of the man's ventricle getting perforated had worn off, leaving a stabbing ache behind. An ache of disappointment that the trial had ultimately not been the success he'd so wanted and expected it to be. An ache for the patient having to recover from this intense surgery, if he did recover.

An ache for Avery, who was long gone to who knew where. And all because he'd refused to listen to her.

Avery not being there, standing next to him through this thing, felt all wrong. How had that happened in a few short weeks? He had no idea, but somehow her absence felt like a huge, gaping hole in his life. In his heart.

All he'd wanted or needed in his life had been his work. Something he loved and was damned good at. Until Avery had shown up. Avery, in her colorful clothes with her beautiful green eyes, a teasing smile on her face and every bit as strong a work ethic as he had.

He'd wanted just a day or two of fun with her. To his surprise, she'd given him that and so much more. And what had he given her? Not a damn thing. Not even the respect he'd slammed her old boyfriend for not giving, either.

He shook his head at himself. What a damn fool.

Hours later, the surgery was over and a success, and Jack could only hope that the man remained in a stable condition. Feeling wiped out, he changed out of his scrubs and went to his hotel room. The thought of going out to eat without Avery sounded miserable, and he didn't feel like hashing out the day's events with Jessica, either. As he pondered room service, a knock at the door sent his heart slamming against his ribs.

Had Avery heard what had happened? He moved toward the door, wishing it would be her standing there, ready to give him another lecture that, for once, he'd be happy to listen to.

But it wasn't. "Jessica."

"Wow, my ego's gotten even bigger at how excited you sound to see me," she mocked. "Can I come in for a minute?"

"I'm always glad to see you. I'm just tired."

"Of course you're tired. I don't think you've rested for more than a few hours all week, and today was rough."

She sat on the side of the bed while Jack perched in the wooden chair by a small table and looked at her. "I've decided to stop the trial. I'm telling Timkin tomorrow morning."

He hadn't even realized he'd made that final decision, but now that the words had come out of his mouth, he knew without a doubt it was the right one.

Jessica nodded. "I figured you would. But that's not what I want to talk to you about."

He raised his eyebrows at her, hoping she didn't have some marital problem with Brandon. He wasn't up for that kind of conversation.

"Are you interested in where Avery Girard is?"

Hell, yes. He sat up straight. "I might be."

"Might be. Right." She snorted. "You've been glum and cranky ever since she quit the trial, even before today's scary event. Which I guess proved maybe she was right, which means maybe you should find her and apologize and kiss her and then we can all be happy again."

If only it were that easy. "I don't think she has much interest in my apologies." Or in his kisses, and the thought made his chest ache all over again.

"I bet she does. But there's only one way for you to find out." She dug into her purse and pulled out a piece of paper, leaning over to wave it in his face. "Her address in Montmartre. She's rented an apartment for the month."

"How did you find that out?"

"Nurses at any hospital know everything." She stood and patted him on the head like he was a little kid. "Now, go. I'm heading to dinner with my cousin and expect a full report tomorrow."

He stared at the door closing behind her as adrenaline surged through his blood.

He knew he'd disappointed Avery, but he could fix that. Tomorrow was Valentine's Day, and he had to admit he didn't know much about romance. But the woman who'd held his clinical trial in her hands held his heart now instead, and she'd given him a few ideas about what just might work on her.

Avery frowned at the knock on her door, wondering who the heck could be bothering her at 9:00 p.m. in an apartment few knew she'd moved into. While she was eating marshmallows and macaroons and crying over movies. Cautiously, she peeked through the peephole and the shock of who was standing there stole her breath.

How had Jack found out where she was? And why? She knew it couldn't have anything to do with it being

Valentine's Day. The man probably wasn't even aware of the holiday.

She took a moment to wipe her nose and eyes, smooth down her skirt and conjure the frustration and deep disappointment she'd felt the last time she'd seen him. Except the sight of his handsome, tired face made her want to wrap her arms around him and hold him close instead.

Disgusted with herself, she opened the door. "Lost in Paris?"

A small smile touched his mouth, but didn't make it to his eyes. "I am lost. Looking for a tour guide. You available?"

"No, I'm not."

"Can you give me just ten minutes? Please?"

She willed herself to resist the entreaty in his beautiful brown eyes, but felt that darned melting sensation inside her chest that seemed to happen whenever he was near. She sighed and figured she may as well spend ten minutes with him. Who knew? Maybe it would help heal the huge hole he'd left in her heart.

"Ten minutes."

She grabbed her coat from the rack by the door, and the feel of his fingers touching the back of her neck as he gently tugged her hair from inside made her eyes sting again. Lord, if she'd known what a heartbreaker the man was, she'd have avoided him that first day in the hotel like flesh-eating bacteria.

A little half laugh, half sob formed in her throat as she thought about their ridiculous conversation about that and snails and about the magical time they'd spent in Riquewihr. Which hadn't accomplished a thing, except to make her fall even harder for the man.

She was a little surprised he didn't touch her the way he always did as they walked to wherever it was they were going. Clearly, this must be a business visit and nothing more. Which, of course, she'd known anyway. Tears again blurred her eyes, and she forcefully blinked them back, getting really annoyed with herself now. Why would it even cross her mind to think it might be anything else?

When her vision cleared, she glanced at her watch, noting the time and fully planning on only ten darned minutes of torture with the man. Then realized they were standing by the Wall of I Love You. As she looked at him in surprise, the memory of kissing him there clogged up her breath.

"Someone told me this was a special place created just for lovers to meet. And this day, of all days of the year, seems like a good one for that to happen." He reached for her hands. "At the time, I thought that was a little hokey. I didn't realize how important such a place could be until my lover left me."

His lover. She closed her eyes at how wonderful that had been. But it wasn't meant to be. "We were supposed to be lovers just that one day. We should have left it that way."

"If that was all it was supposed to be, it would have been. But it was more than that. A whole lot more, at least for me. You brought a joy into my life I didn't even know was missing."

His words, the intense way he was staring at her squeezed her heart. But what was she supposed to say to that? He had his work and she had hers, and trying to combine that with being lovers had created nothing but conflict and pain.

"I love you, Avery." His hands tightened on hers. "I thought my work could be everything. But now I know. Even if I never see you again, it will never be enough. There would always be an empty place where you belong."

He loved her? Stunned, she stared at him as he drew her close, wrapped his arms around her and kissed her. So sure she'd never feel his lips on hers again, the pleasure of it had her melting into his chest and sighing into his mouth.

He pulled back slightly to look at her. "Remember when we made a wish at the fountain? I got my wish."

"I know. I figured you wished for sex, except I was going to give you that anyway."

"No, though I wasn't counting on that. Just hoping." A small smile touched his lips before he got serious again. "I wished for the wisdom to know when to keep at something and when to quit. It didn't kick in any too soon, but thank God it finally did."

"You're stopping the trial?"

"Yes. I'm sorry I didn't listen to you, because I should have. But that's not what I got the wisdom for. My wish kicked in when I knew I had to find you and tell you how much I love you and ask you to forgive me for all the things I've done wrong."

"You...you're not still mad about me not telling you the truth?"

"I wish you'd been honest with me, but who knows? Maybe we would have really kept our distance from one another, and we wouldn't be standing here tonight, kissing, on Valentine's Day."

"Maybe you're right. Who knew you were such a romantic?" Swallowing back tears, she reached to cup his face in her hand, barely believing this was really happening.

His lips curved in his first real smile of the night, and he gave her a long, delicious kiss that wobbled her knees before he let her go and reached into his pocket. To her shock, he pulled out the music box she'd looked at with him. The little tune tinkled when he opened it, and she started to shake all over when she saw what was inside it.

"Jack. What—"

"You said you wanted to be draped in gold." His fingers grasped the ring tucked into the red velvet folds of the box and held it up. A diamond flanked by sapphires, rubies and emeralds. "I thought a plain diamond was too dull for you, and I'm not sure this qualifies as draping, except around your finger. But I hope it's good enough for now. Will you marry me and be my forever Valentine, Avery?"

"You're asking me to marry you?" She stared into the intense brown of his eyes, barely breathing.

"I'm asking you to marry me. Begging. And since I'm about to have a heart attack because you haven't said you love me, too, please tell me. One way or the other."

"The answer is yes. *Oui, oui, oui.* And I do love you. Crazily love you. Wildly love you."

"Insanely love *you*." He pulled her close and pressed his face to her hair. "I don't deserve you, but I'm keeping you anyway." He held her for a long time before sliding the ring onto her shaking finger. She sniffed at the tears stupidly popping into her eyes again and wished she could see it better.

He held her hand tight as he pressed soft kisses down her cheek. "What do you say we team up to create a new TAVI device, Dr. Girard?" he whispered against her skin. "Sound like a good idea?"

"Une très bonne idée." She tunneled her hands into his hair and tipped his face so she could look into his beautiful eyes. Eyes that looked at her with the same kind of love she felt all but bursting from her chest. "I think we'll make a very good team, Dr. Dunbar. One very good team."

* * * * *

MILLS & BOON®
Hardback – February 2015

ROMANCE

The Redemption of Darius Sterne	Carole Mortimer
The Sultan's Harem Bride	Annie West
Playing by the Greek's Rules	Sarah Morgan
Innocent in His Diamonds	Maya Blake
To Wear His Ring Again	Chantelle Shaw
The Man to Be Reckoned With	Tara Pammi
Claimed by the Sheikh	Rachael Thomas
Delucca's Marriage Contract	Abby Green
Her Brooding Italian Boss	Susan Meier
The Heiress's Secret Baby	Jessica Gilmore
A Pregnancy, a Party & a Proposal	Teresa Carpenter
Best Friend to Wife and Mother?	Caroline Anderson
The Sheikh Doctor's Bride	Meredith Webber
A Baby to Heal Their Hearts	Kate Hardy
One Hot Desert Night	Kristi Gold
Snowed In with Her Ex	Andrea Laurence
Cowgirls Don't Cry	Silver James
Terms of a Texas Marriage	Lauren Canan

MEDICAL

A Date with Her Valentine Doc	Melanie Milburne
It Happened in Paris...	Robin Gianna
Temptation in Paradise	Joanna Neil
The Surgeon's Baby Secret	Amber McKenzie

MILLS & BOON®
Large Print – February 2015

ROMANCE

An Heiress for His Empire	Lucy Monroe
His for a Price	Caitlin Crews
Commanded by the Sheikh	Kate Hewitt
The Valquez Bride	Melanie Milburne
The Uncompromising Italian	Cathy Williams
Prince Hafiz's Only Vice	Susanna Carr
A Deal Before the Altar	Rachael Thomas
The Billionaire in Disguise	Soraya Lane
The Unexpected Honeymoon	Barbara Wallace
A Princess by Christmas	Jennifer Faye
His Reluctant Cinderella	Jessica Gilmore

HISTORICAL

Zachary Black: Duke of Debauchery	Carole Mortimer
The Truth About Lady Felkirk	Christine Merrill
The Courtesan's Book of Secrets	Georgie Lee
Betrayed by His Kiss	Amanda McCabe
Falling for Her Captor	Elisabeth Hobbes

MEDICAL

Tempted by Her Boss	Scarlet Wilson
His Girl From Nowhere	Tina Beckett
Falling For Dr Dimitriou	Anne Fraser
Return of Dr Irresistible	Amalie Berlin
Daring to Date Her Boss	Joanna Neil
A Doctor to Heal Her Heart	Annie Claydon

MILLS & BOON®
Hardback – March 2015

ROMANCE

The Taming of Xander Sterne	Carole Mortimer
In the Brazilian's Debt	Susan Stephens
At the Count's Bidding	Caitlin Crews
The Sheikh's Sinful Seduction	Dani Collins
The Real Romero	Cathy Williams
His Defiant Desert Queen	Jane Porter
Prince Nadir's Secret Heir	Michelle Conder
Princess's Secret Baby	Carol Marinelli
The Renegade Billionaire	Rebecca Winters
The Playboy of Rome	Jennifer Faye
Reunited with Her Italian Ex	Lucy Gordon
Her Knight in the Outback	Nikki Logan
Baby Twins to Bind Them	Carol Marinelli
The Firefighter to Heal Her Heart	Annie O'Neil
Thirty Days to Win His Wife	Andrea Laurence
Her Forbidden Cowboy	Charlene Sands
The Blackstone Heir	Dani Wade
After Hours with Her Ex	Maureen Child

MEDICAL

Tortured by Her Touch	Dianne Drake
It Happened in Vegas	Amy Ruttan
The Family She Needs	Sue MacKay
A Father for Poppy	Abigail Gordon

MILLS & BOON®
Large Print – March 2015

ROMANCE

A Virgin for His Prize	Lucy Monroe
The Valquez Seduction	Melanie Milburne
Protecting the Desert Princess	Carol Marinelli
One Night with Morelli	Kim Lawrence
To Defy a Sheikh	Maisey Yates
The Russian's Acquisition	Dani Collins
The True King of Dahaar	Tara Pammi
The Twelve Dates of Christmas	Susan Meier
At the Chateau for Christmas	Rebecca Winters
A Very Special Holiday Gift	Barbara Hannay
A New Year Marriage Proposal	Kate Hardy

HISTORICAL

Darian Hunter: Duke of Desire	Carole Mortimer
Rescued by the Viscount	Anne Herries
The Rake's Bargain	Lucy Ashford
Unlaced by Candlelight	Various
The Warrior's Winter Bride	Denise Lynn

MEDICAL

A Secret Shared...	Marion Lennox
Flirting with the Doc of Her Dreams	Janice Lynn
The Doctor Who Made Her Love Again	Susan Carlisle
The Maverick Who Ruled Her Heart	Susan Carlisle
After One Forbidden Night...	Amber McKenzie
Dr Perfect on Her Doorstep	Lucy Clark

0215 GEN STD LP

MILLS & BOON®

Why shop at millsandboon.co.uk?

Each year, thousands of romance readers find their perfect read at millsandboon.co.uk. That's because we're passionate about bringing you the very best romantic fiction. Here are some of the advantages of shopping at www.millsandboon.co.uk:

* **Get new books first**—you'll be able to buy your favourite books one month before they hit the shops

* **Get exclusive discounts**—you'll also be able to buy our specially created monthly collections, with up to 50% off the RRP

* **Find your favourite authors**—latest news, interviews and new releases for all your favourite authors and series on our website, plus ideas for what to try next

* **Join in**—once you've bought your favourite books, don't forget to register with us to rate, review and join in the discussions

Visit **www.millsandboon.co.uk**
for all this and more today!